A DEADLY BARGAIN— PLAN C

A DEADLY BARGAIN— PLAN C

•

Gina Cresse

AVALON BOOKS
NEW YORK

MYS
C 9222dc

PRINTED IN THE UNITED STATES OF AMERICA
ON ACID-FREE PAPER
BY HADDON CRAFTSMEN, BLOOMSBURG, PENNSYLVANIA

This is the page where I get to thank all those who helped me get this story down on paper. Not only are they really smart people with more expertise in their fields than I could ever hope to have, but also dear friends and family, whose support and encouragement gave me the energy to burn the *midnight-oil*.

Thanks to: my dad, Larry Cresse, the smartest man I know; Jim and Iva Lou Woodring, for giving me a little insight into the California Department of Justice; Michael Strohmaier, the brightest computer techno-wizard (without a pocket protector) this side of the Mississippi; my sister, Terese Knapp, for taking the research trip with me to Catalina Island; Sandy Taylor, for making sure I dotted my 'i's and crossed my t's'; Doug Richards, Erin Cartwright, and Veronica Mixon, for giving me a reality check whenever I drifted into left field; and to whoever is responsible for the World Wide Web.

Chapter One

Roy Hastings cut the single Detroit-diesel engine on his 45-foot Fort Pierce dive boat. The storm winds, already whipping with menacing force, beat the rain against his unshaven face like the jabs of a thousand tiny darts.

He set out from Avalon Harbor as soon as he got word of the storm—bound and determined not to let this stinkin' *El Niño* take his precious *Little Maria,* the way *The Sweet Life* was claimed back in '82.

Not that the *Little Maria* was anything elaborate or notably valuable—at least in the eyes of a marine-craft appraiser. As boats go, she was as common as they come. *She's functional,* Roy remembered thinking to himself the day he bought her. She'd carry all the divers, fishermen, and equipment he needed on chartered trips. She didn't offer any sleeping quarters, fancy furniture, or shiny chrome and brass points, but she did have a modest galley and a head—that certainly counted for something. No, an appraiser wouldn't put the same value on her that Roy did. To him, she was more than a boat, much more. She gave him independence; she gave him freedom to do what he loved. She gave him life. In his eyes, she was priceless.

He finished tying the last bowline in a nylon rope

1

and struggled to keep a tight hold on the sea anchor attached to it. The wind caught the parachute-like device and threatened to carry it, along with Roy, over the railing into the nine-foot swells waiting to swallow the vessel in one giant gulp. In the past, Roy used an old surplus parachute to keep his bow into the wind, but this storm gave him a bad feeling. After the devil-sent storms of '82 beat his boat against the rocks until it splintered into a thousand pieces, Roy took to weathering the storms at sea. He'd take his chances and go down with the ship if it came to that, but he wasn't about to let the elements take his only means of livelihood again—not without a fight.

The brand-new, bright-red nylon anchor whipped in the wind and the hardware beat against his arms and chest. He swore under his breath and shook his fist at the gloomy, black sky. When he finally had the lines secured, he hurled the big, awkward thing overboard and watched the wind catch it, like a drag-chute on a racecar. The anchor settled itself on the surface, then sank slowly into the turbulent seas. When the water rose up over his head, he saw the red fabric lurk in the swells, like the tongue of a giant, boat-eating monster.

He raised his face and scowled at the black clouds that loomed overhead, preying on the *Little Maria.* "You're not gettin' this one!" he swore.

The deck pitched and rolled with the huge swells. Roy clung to the rail as he made his way to the cabin door. A lightning strike off the port side, followed by a clap of thunder, shook him in his shoes. He lost his grip on the rail and fell to the deck. He climbed back to his feet and reached for the door handle. Opening the door, he remembered he'd left his only pair of binoculars on the flybridge. He considered leaving them there to fend for themselves, but common sense reminded him he'd need them. He closed the door and hiked his jacket collar up around his neck to keep the rain from running down his back.

He set one foot on the first rung of the slippery ladder and then climbed. Halfway up, his foot slipped, and he banged his shin on the hard metal bar. Though he was cold and numb, he was sure it drew blood. He cursed again.

The binoculars slipped off the console and landed under the pilot seat. Roy picked them up, held them to his wind-beaten face, and scanned the roller-coaster horizon. When the *Little Maria* reached the top of the swell, he spotted a yacht in the distance, off the port side. Then his boat fell to the bottom of the wave, and he lost sight of the vessel. He waited for the crest of the swell five more times to get a good look at the neighboring yacht, then made his way down to the shelter of the cabin.

The yacht must have been at least a hundred-footer, maybe even bigger, from the looks of it. *Some fancy yacht for sure,* Roy thought to himself. *They must be out there weathering the storm, same as me.*

He shed his soaked windbreaker and grabbed a towel from the head to dry his drenched hair. "Long night," he said to himself as he peered out the window and cringed at the solid wall of water facing him.

It was nearly three in the morning before the storm finally subsided. Exhausted, Roy peeled off his soaked clothes and slipped into a pair of dry jeans and a zip-up sweatshirt. He poured a cup of hot coffee from a thermos, but fell asleep before he took the first sip.

Roy woke, still sitting at the galley table with his head resting on his folded arms. The sun peeked through the porthole and caught him square in the eyes.

He stepped onto the deck and smiled at the clear sky. "Told ya you couldn't have her, didn't I!"

He inspected the condition of the *Little Maria*. The radio antenna cable dangled in the breeze without an antenna, but she was still afloat—that was most important.

The water, calm and smooth as glass, was a far cry from the horrible monster of the night before. Roy hauled in the sea anchor and spread it out on the deck to dry. He climbed up to the flybridge and scanned the horizon for the yacht he'd seen the night before. She was nowhere in sight.

"Hmm. Probably off to Mexico, by now."

Roy took one last look in the direction of the mysterious boat, then fired up his engine. It would take almost two hours to get back to Avalon Harbor on Catalina Island—back to the safety of the marina.

He'd been cruising along for forty-five minutes, when something floating in the water caught his eye. He cut back the throttle and motored up to it. A white deck chair drifted by his bow. Then another. A closer inspection of the area revealed a half-dozen seat cushions, ten adult-sized life jackets, a first-aid kit, and a [Jim Buoy] throw ring. Something odd bobbed in the water about ten yards away. Roy approached, squinting to focus on the dozen-or-so items floating by his port side. They were flat, about eight-inches square, black and white, and marked sort of like a holstein cow.

"What the heck?" Roy fished one of the strange objects from the water. The small, plastic mat dripped a few spots of water on his shoe as he shook it.

Roy opened his equipment trunk and tossed the curious item inside, resigned to discover its purpose in life later, after he made a more thorough search of the area.

He drifted slowly around the area, his eyes trained on the depth sounder's video screen. The bright red, yellow, and green, on the deep-blue background formed abstract shapes, indicating the contours of the bottom. Roy knew the geometry of the shape he stared at wasn't a natural occurrence. There was something down there.

Roy dropped his anchor and watched as the nylon rope fed itself into the waiting water.

"Hmm. Hundred and fifty feet. Pretty deep."

He went below and checked the gauges on the scuba tanks in the racks. He pulled one out and hauled it up to the deck. He unlocked a trunk, sitting on the deck, and pulled out the rest of his diving gear. He peeled off his bulky jeans and sweatshirt, then squeezed into the rubber wet suit.

Roy hooked his underwater camera and flashlight to his dive belt, adjusted his mouthpiece, and pulled his mask over his face. He pushed himself backward over the rail and splashed into the unusually-warm Pacific water.

He descended as quickly as was safe. It didn't take long for his powerful flashlight to locate the brilliant-white paint of the S.M. Italian Motoryacht. Roy checked his watch. In one hundred and fifty feet, he could only dive the wreck for about ten minutes.

The yacht was beautiful—built in the early to mid-nineties, by Roy's estimation. He unhooked the camera from his belt and snapped pictures of the scene. He checked his watch, then slithered through the salon doorway to get a look inside. Even in the dark murky water, the overstuffed sofas, plush carpeting, expensively framed paintings, and a bank of electronic equipment that would have put an aircraft carrier to shame, made it clear this was no poor-man's toy.

Roy checked his watch again. He didn't have much time left. He located the hatch to get below deck and slipped through the opening. Some containers were stacked along the edges of the hold; Roy knew they must be water-tight because they pressed against the ceiling, trying to float to the surface.

Roy's interest in the floating containers didn't last long, once he'd looked past them. Staring in amazement at the sight, Roy shook his head in disbelief. He checked his camera—only two frames left. He snapped them both, then looked at his watch. His time was up. He began his ascent back to the surface.

The GPS-99P, one of the best investments Roy made last year, could store two hundred and thirty latitude/longitude positions, allowing him to keep track of all his favorite diving and fishing spots. He punched in the identifier, "elninowreck," and saved the date, time, and location in the electronic navigation system.

Roy took one last look at the floating debris, fired up his engine, and headed for home.

*   *   *

Roy tied the *Little Maria* to her designated buoy. He loaded a tank cart and two dive tanks into his dinghy and motored it to the dock. He removed the equipment from the small boat and headed up the wooden walkway toward Sherman's Dive Shop. The wheels of the cart squeaked as they rolled behind him. In his free hand, he carried the strange rubber mat he'd found floating near the wreck site. Busy studying the words on the mat, he almost walked into a man coming from the other direction. "Oh! Pardon me," Roy apologized.

"No problem," the man replied. He stepped aside to let Roy pass.

Roy and Sherman had been friends for nearly fifteen years. Sherman arranged most of Roy's charters, for a small commission. The business relationship was a good one for them both.

The big cowbell hanging on the dive shop door clanked as Roy pushed it open. Sherman glanced up as Roy strolled in.

"Hey, Sherm. How'd you make out in that storm?"

Sherman put his fingers on his wrist to check his pulse. "Let's see. Yeah, blood's still pumpin', if that's what you mean. But my boat's seen better days. Got a big ol' hole in her hull."

"Sorry to hear it."

"I'll tell ya, I'd rather risk losing the boat, while I sit in my living room and watch Titanic videos, than face a storm like that one last night," Sherman barked.

"Why, you're nothing but a chicken, Sherman."

"Ain't denying it. Cluck, cluck."

The two men laughed.

A newspaper was spread out on the counter in front

of Sherman. "Hey. You hear about Otis? He caught a marlin up north of Frisco. You believe that? A marlin. Said the water's so warm, they're catching all kinds of strange fish. *El Niño,* ya know," Sherman said.

"Did you actually see it? You know Otis; he's so full of it. I never saw anyone could exaggerate a fish story better than that old coot."

"He ain't tellin' no fish story this time. Look here. It's in today's paper. There's a picture and everything."

Sherman clipped the photo and caption from the newspaper and tacked it to the corkboard on the wall behind the counter.

"Well, just wait till you see the pictures I'll have to show. *El Niño's* up to more than just misplacing a few fish. You'll never guess what I found while I was out there. Some poor, or I should say, rich, son-of-a-gun lost a beautiful yacht in that storm."

"You don't say. Everyone okay?"

"Don't know. No sign of people. Just some deck furniture—usual stuff—except for this thing." Roy held out the small rubber mat he'd fished out of the water. "Any idea what this here is?"

Sherman took it and shook his head. "Roy! Don't you know a mouse pad when you see one?"

"Mouse pad? What the heck's a mouse pad? Some kind of new trap?"

"I swear, Roy. I'm gonna get you caught up to the twentieth century, if it kills me. 'Course, by that time, we'll be in the twenty-first, and you'll be way behind *again.* A mouse pad's for a computer mouse to move around on. Has a little track-ball inside that needs a clean, smooth surface. Haven't you seen me use mine?"

"Yeah, I've seen it, but didn't know what it was. Why the heck's it called a mouse?"

" 'Cause, Roy, it sort of looks like a mouse, with a long ol' tail. See?" Sherman dangled the small, plastic device by its cord in front of Roy's face.

"Hmm. Too big to be a mouse. How come they don't call it a rat? It's more the size of a rat. And, a rat has a longer tail."

"Now, think about it, Roy. You really think people would want to grab hold of something called a rat?"

"Not any more than they'd want to squeeze their fingers around a mouse, I suppose."

Sherman laughed and shook his head. "Guess you've got a point. Anyhow, tell me about this wreck. What happened?"

"Really weird. Boat like that shouldn't have had any problem in last night's storm; there was something fishy about it. I need to call the Coast Guard to report it. Can I use your phone?"

"Phones are out on the whole island. Storm wiped 'em out last night. Probably won't have service back till tomorrow, late. What about your radio?"

"Out of commission. Gotta pick up a new antenna," Roy answered.

A customer, busy inspecting a rack of snorkel equipment, perked up his ears at the conversation. He set down the mask and walked to the counter. "You say you saw a boat sink?"

Roy turned around to see who spoke. It was the man he'd nearly run over on the sidewalk. "Well, I didn't actually see it go down. I saw the yacht last night during the storm. Then, this morning, I found stuff floating and decided to take a look. She was the same boat, alright—sitting on the bottom in a hundred fifty feet of saltwater."

"That's pretty far down. You must be the divemaster" the stranger said.

"One and the same. Roy Hastings—certified and all—the whole shebang."

"Certifiable, you mean," Sherman jested. "Anyone crazy enough to set out alone against last night's storm must have one oar out of the water."

"Hey, I'm still vertical, aren't I?" Roy defended. "Anyhow, look who's talking. Any *man* who wears his hair in a ponytail, especially after his sixtieth birthday, must have *both* oars not only out of the water, but probably on another boat."

The stranger chuckled at the banter between the two buddies, then held his hand out to Roy. "Kent Morrison."

Roy shook his hand.

"I'd like to take a look at that boat. Could you find it again?" Morrison asked.

"Sure. But you gotta be certified to make a dive like that."

"Oh, I've got a certificate. Used to dive for the Navy. Seen more of this world under water, than I've seen on dry land."

"Really? Well, okay. Tomorrow alright for you? I'm in desperate need of some food, a shave, and a good night's sleep."

"I'll be here. Six o'clock okay?"

"That'll be fine. And bring that certificate," Roy reminded him.

"Sure thing."

Kent followed Roy toward the exit. Halfway out the door, Roy stopped and snapped his fingers. He stuck his head back into the shop. "Oh, Sherm. I left a couple tanks in the back. Can you fill them for me? I'll need them for tomorrow's dive."

"I'll have 'em ready for the morning. But I won't be out of bed by six. I'll leave 'em out for you."

"Thanks."

Kent had his gear all ready to go in front of the dive shop when Roy arrived. Kent. He was as anxious as a kid on Christmas Eve.

"Coffee?" Roy said offering a thermos to his newest customer.

"No, thanks. Don't drink it."

Roy shot a skeptical glance at Kent. "Don't know if I trust a man who doesn't drink coffee."

Kent chuckled. "We all set to go? Can't wait to see this wreck. Did I hear you say you took pictures?"

"Yeah. Come on. Dinghy's tied up at the end of the dock. You bring that certificate?"

"You betcha."

Roy set a big blue ice chest on the deck. "You can stow your gear over there." He pointed to a rack designed to hold the bulky oxygen tanks.

"How long till we get there?" Kent asked.

"About an hour. There are sodas and sandwiches in that ice chest. Donuts and juice, too. Help yourself," Roy offered.

"Thanks."

Roy disappeared into the cabin. Within five

minutes, the diesel engine rumbled, and they were on their way. Roy punched in the "elninowreck" identifier on his GPS and let it lead him to the exact spot.

When they arrived at the wreck site, Roy cut the engine and dropped anchor.

"Here we are," Roy announced.

"This is it?"

"Yep. Ready to gear up?"

"You betcha! I'm just gonna use the head."

While Kent went below to use the facilities, Roy pulled one of the newly-filled tanks from his rack and checked the gauge. It didn't indicate full. "Hmm. Leaky valve," he speculated.

Roy opened his equipment trunk and laid the defective tank on its side, then closed and locked the box. He hung the ring of keys on a hook just inside the cabin.

Kent returned to the deck, drying his hands on his jacket. "You're out of towels down there."

"Sorry. I'll stock up when we get back."

As Kent sorted through his gear, he glanced at Roy. "I didn't bring my camera. Think we could use yours to take some more shots? I'd sure like to get a few pictures."

"Out of film. I meant to pick up some rolls last night, but I didn't get to it."

"Too bad. What kind of camera do you use?" Kent asked.

"Nikon. F3, I think. Pretty nice piece of equipment."

The two men squeezed into their wet suits and hoisted the heavy tanks onto their backs.

Roy recited a brief set of safety guidelines that he expected all his customers to follow. Kent nodded, understanding the rules, and then followed Roy over the edge of the *Little Maria*.

Within three minutes of the dive, Roy knew something was wrong. His vision blurred and he felt light-headed. He was nauseous and knew he needed to get to the surface. He touched Kent on the arm and pointed up with his thumb. Kent shook his head and continued down. Roy, about to pass out, signaled again. Kent refused to follow. He continued descending on the wreck.

Roy watched him for a moment, then the world went dark. He shook his head to clear his vision. *It can't be the bends,* he thought to himself. He tried to release his weight belt, but his arms and legs were limp. He coughed out his mouthpiece and took his last breath.

Kent watched, unmoved, as Roy lost consciousness. He checked his watch and began his ascent to the surface. He knew he had little time to get Roy's boat to the prearranged *rendezvous* to meet up with the others.

At first, Kent was barely startled by the light bump he felt on his back. His line of work demanded nerves of steel in tense situations. He was preoccupied, looking at the frayed ends of the line dangling from above. Something had cut or chewed the rope and freed the *Little Maria* from its anchor. He turned to see what had run into him in the dark water—facing him were the open jaws of a Great White, ready to close around his body.

Chapter Two

I set out at the crack of dawn yesterday morning on a mission . . . no . . . more like a pilgrimage, to Long Beach Harbor. My destination: Tex and Clancy's Marine Salvage, Pier S, Berth 19.

I'd read a notice in the legal section of the *San Diego Union-Tribune* last Sunday. Tex and Clancy's Marine Salvage posted a notice of intent to apply for title to an abandoned vessel they'd found six months ago. It's not that I'm interested in claiming the boat; what intrigues me is that this Tex and Clancy outfit can just take ownership of the vessel, providing no one shows up to claim it. What a sweet deal. They scout around the Pacific all day, treasure hunting, the same as me—only I generally focus on probate sales, foreclosed storage units, yard sales, flea markets, and swap meets.

When I read the notice, my eyes lit up, and I got all excited—like the time I bought a Taylor guitar at the Saugus Speedway swap meet for one hundred and twenty dollars. The next weekend, I sold it for fifteen hundred. This marine salvage could open up a whole new avenue of potential revenue. I just love this business.

My name is Devonie Lace, and if you haven't

guessed by now, I belong to a special group known as self-employed treasure hunters. I chose this profession after discovering that I'm a square peg in a world that consists of nothing but round holes. The world kept trying to file off my edges, to make me round, so I would fit. It didn't work. I decided it would be better to go in search of some square holes.

The *Plan C* is a sixty-five-foot sailing yacht that I absolutely adore (except when I have to maneuver her around other boats, docks, piers, or islands. Someone once told me I couldn't sail a boat this size by myself. When I was six, my brother told me I could never climb the big oak tree in our backyard. That's what I told the fireman as he carried me down the ladder to my worried mother's arms. Don't tell me I can't do something.

She's a beauty, but steering her is like trying to push a cooked noodle through a bowl of oatmeal. I sweat bullets every time I come within fifty feet of another boat—heck, within fifty feet of *anything,* besides water.

Just my luck, today, of all days, would be the first-annual, Long Beach Amateur Sailor Regatta, with floating parade to follow. My stomach was in knots.

As I approached Long Beach Harbor, beads of sweat formed on my forehead. I counted the huge freighters I'd have to get around along with what looked like about a thousand boaters out for a day on the water. I wondered if I could feign mechanical trouble and convince the harbor patrol to tow me in with one of those cute little tugboats.

When I passed the small concrete lighthouse, marking the mouth of the harbor, I dropped my sails and assessed the minefield in front of me. My first obstacle would be a huge freighter, off to the left—I mean port—side of my boat. That shouldn't be too hard to miss—it's only about a bazillion feet long and weighs just as much. Hitting it would be like running head-long into Iceland or Tasmania.

I started my engine and inched the throttle ever-so-gently to the little picture of a turtle, which I had pasted to the console.

People in small crafts persisted in crossing my path, completely oblivious to the fact that I had very little—okay, absolutely no—control of this wide-body, super-sized, double-length, Greyhound-bus-like vessel of which I claim to be the skipper. I waved my arms frantically and yelled, "Not so close! I'm carrying nuclear waste!" to a party boat that wandered into my trajectory.

They all smiled and waved back to me, holding up their beers and hollering, "So are we!"

I held my breath as they inched out of my way, just as I crossed their wake.

The big, red-and-white public transportation boat to Catalina Island, or the cattle boat, as the locals like to call it, headed directly for me. For the life of me, I couldn't remember the rule here. Do I yield? Or do they? Do I pass on the port or starboard side?

I put my hand on the throttle and pulled it back. Not a good move. Now I drifted, unable to steer at all. I'd either have to drop my anchor or start moving again. I pushed the lever back up to the turtle and jumped when the oncoming boat's alarm-like-horn blared at me. Apparently, I'm required to yield to them. I turned the wheel starboard, hoping that would be the correct action. The pilot of the cattle boat shook his head, as we passed within feet of each other.

"Why didn't I just drive my Jeep?" I asked myself, as I smiled and waved to the aggravated boat pilot. He waved back, but he wasn't smiling. Actually, I'm not sure you could consider the gesture he gave me a wave; it was more of a fist-shaking.

Flustered, I returned my attention to the challenge at hand: getting from point A to point B without hitting any of the moving obstacles—on the stationary ones—in between. I checked the signs marking the piers and searched for the correct one. Finally, I spotted "Pier S" and turned the wheel toward it.

I studied the size of the openings on the dock and peered down the length of the *Plan C*. I shut one eye and looked again, biting my lip.

"Oh, heck. I've got that perfectly good dinghy. May as well use it," I convinced myself. I cut the engine and dropped my anchor right where I sat.

I went below to get my purse. The scent from a dozen red roses sitting on the galley table, beautifully arranged in a glass vase, wafted to my nose. I stopped and gazed at them. What would I do about those roses? I sat down for a moment and played with the petals that had dropped to the table. They felt soft and velvety. I pulled another from the blossom and held it to my nose. I squeezed my eyes shut. "Darn you, Craig," I whispered. "Everything was so simple. Why'd you have to complicate it?" I tossed the petal in the trash and climbed back to the deck.

A group of sailors on a nearby fishing boat watched with amusement as I struggled to start the little outboard motor on my dinghy. I yanked the cord. Nothing. I pulled again, lost my balance, and almost fell overboard.

Finally, one of the smart alecks called over to me: "Did you switch on the gas?"

I smiled at him, as I slid back off the edge of the dinghy. "Yeah. It's just cold."

"You sure? Need some help?"

"No, thanks. I'll get it," I insisted.

The crew watched me for a while. I sat on the small bench and worked diligently at tying my shoes, filing a snag on my fingernail, removing a loose thread from my shorts, inspecting an old scar on my knee, and cleaning my sunglasses. I glanced over at the fishing boat. They'd tired of waiting for me to take a graceful swan dive into the drink and turned their attention to some other form of amusement: a baseball game on the radio. I nonchalantly reached over and flipped the fuel switch to the "On" position. I fired up the motor and proceeded toward the dock. I passed close to the group of sailors. One smiled and winked at me, holding his finger over his lips. My secret was safe with him.

I eased the little craft to the dock and tied up next to another boat—about a forty-or forty-five-footer, I guessed. Looked like some kind of commercial boat, probably for fishing or diving charters. Nothing fancy, just practical. I made a mental note of the workhorse's name *Little Maria*.

Chapter Three

A huge golden retriever came trotting down the dock to greet me, tail wagging, happy as a kid with a new best friend. A red bandana was tied around his neck and a collection of round metal tags hung from his collar. I reached down and patted his big head.

"Well, hello there." I fingered through the tags on his collar in search of his name. "Los Angeles County dog license, Long Beach Veterinary Clinic rabies tag, fishing license?" I chuckled. "Let's see, here's one. Texaco. Is that your name? Texaco?"

The big dog wagged his tail even harder and let out one affirmative bark; then he turned, ran up the dock, retrieved a yellow tennis ball from a bucket, brought it back, and dropped it at my feet.

"Oh, you want to play. Okay." I picked up the ball and tossed it a few yards up the dock.

"What kind of sissy throw was that?" A gruff voice came from inside a small, shack-like structure, with a beat-up sign designating it as the office of "Tex and Clancy's Marine Salvage."

A salty old codger meandered out into the sunshine, as he scratched the gray stubble on his face. The large man wore an old pair of denim overalls with a thread-bare T-shirt underneath. A logo, barely visible on the faded blue shirt, showed the image of a whale and some words I couldn't make out. His gray hair was cut in a butch with a top so flat he could probably sit in my dinghy in a storm, balance a shot of whiskey on his head, and never spill a drop. A large hole in the toe of his red-and-white-plaid deck shoes, revealed that he didn't wear any socks. A red bandana, like the one around Texaco's neck, hung out of his back pocket. He pulled the cloth from his pocket and wiped some grease off his hands; though too late to keep the black smudges off his face where he'd rubbed it.

"Ain't you ever thrown a ball for a dog before?"

"Well, yes. I just didn't want it to go in the water. Then he'd lose it."

"Aw, heck," he grumbled. He picked up the ball and threw it a hard, eighty feet out into the harbor. Texaco took off at a full gallop, made a flying leap off the dock, and swam for his prized toy. Once he grabbed it in his big mouth, he turned and made a beeline for a ramp-like structure at the end of the pier that allowed him to get back on the dock. I watched as the hundred-pound animal barreled up the walkway toward us, water flying in all directions. He stopped dead in his tracks at the man's feet, dropped the ball, took one step back, and shook four gallons of saltwater out of his coat, drenching the man.

"Dang it, Tex! You know I hate when you do that." He dried the spay from his arms with the bandana. "That's enough swimmin' for one day. You go put your toy away."

I watched, incredulously, as the dog picked up the ball, trotted up the dock, and dropped it in a bucket next to the office.

"That wouldn't be Tex, of Tex and Clancy's Marine Salvage, would it?" I asked.

"It most surely would. Who's wantin' to know, anyways?"

"I'm Devonie Lace. You must be Clancy?"

"Bright girl. Better cover you up, so the sun can shine." He held out his half-dried hand for me to shake. "Clancy McGreggor, at your service. What can I do you for—Devonie, you say?"

"That's right. Devonie Lace. I read your notice in the San Diego paper—the one about the abandoned vessel you found."

He scrutinized me. "You ain't the owner, are ya?"

"No. Just curious about the boat, and your business."

He squinted at me. "Devonie. What kind of name is Devonie? Don't believe I ever heard that before."

I flashed him my most charming smile. "My grandfather's name was Devon. After he died, my parents wanted to name their next son after him. Only I came on the scene with all the wrong parts, so they added the 'ie', and there you have it: Devonie."

"Huh? Whatever. Sure you ain't with the marshall's office?"

"No, sir. I'm a treasure hunter, just like you."

Clancy burst out in a loud laugh. "Treasure hunter? What gives you the idea I'm a treasure hunter?"

"Don't you scout around all day, looking for stuff that others might consider wrecks or junk and try to turn a profit on it?"

"I do that, some. Mostly, I go out looking for non-skilled, half-wit, common-senseless sailors who get themselves up to their eyebrows in saltwater predicaments and need to be rescued, towed, slapped silly, and scolded."

I bit my lip and stared down at the toe of my deck shoe, which was busy tracing the seam of a plank. I hoped he hadn't witnessed my entrance into the harbor and my near collision with the cattle boat. "So, you rescue these people, and they pay you?"

"Yep. Most of 'em, anyway. Sometimes I gotta convince 'em my services are worth the fee. Sometimes I can't convince 'em. Sometimes, I keep their boats," he said, a wide smile spread across his face.

"Is that what happened with this one?" I pointed to the *Little Maria,* tied next to my dinghy.

Clancy looked at me through those squinting eyes, again. "You kidding? A boat like that? Person could make a darn good living with that boat. No one in his right mind would let some marine salvager claim it for a measly award. Ain't a thing wrong with her. Just found her abandoned, out about ten miles off Catalina."

I looked the boat over from bow to stern. He was right; not a thing wrong with it that I could see. "Isn't that a little strange? Why would someone just up and leave it?"

"Got me. I'd bet the guy was out diving alone and ran into a school of sharks. Craziest thing in the world, to dive alone. Never know what you're gonna run into out there."

"How awful. Sharks, you think?"

"Could be. Probably never know for sure."

"So you just find a boat like this out at sea, tow it in, and, if no one claims it, it's yours?"

"Well, sort of. Ain't quite that simple. Lots of pro-cedures you gotta go through."

"What sort of procedures?"

"First of all, you gotta wait six months before you can do anything. Then you gotta make an honest effort to find the owner. That's what the notice in the paper was about. If no one shows up after thirty days, you apply for a certificate of title. You pay any fees that are due, and, providin' you ain't made anyone mad at you down at the Commission Office, you become the new mama."

"Cool." I felt the rush of treasure-hunter blood race through my veins. "I guess no one has shown up to claim this one?"

"Not yet. Got one more day before I can file my application. Had me nervous, when you showed up asking about her. Thought for sure you were gonna tell me your name was Maria, and she was named after you."

"Sorry I put a scare in you. Mind if I take a look at her?"

Clancy scratched his stubbly chin and eyed me again. "S'pose it couldn't hurt, if you just wanna look. I better show you around, though, so you don't get in any trouble."

We climbed over the rail and toured the deck of the boat. There were no frills here. Just a no-nonsense, practical vessel with a job to do. No fancy drink hold-ers, no elaborate stereo system, no polished brass or chrome, no plush reclining deck chairs, no sleeping quarters . . . nothing like my *Plan C*.

A large trunk, shoved under a bench in the corner

of the deck, caught my eye. A big, rusty lock secured the latch.

"What's in the trunk?" I asked.

Clancy scratched his head. "Don't know. Ain't looked."

"You haven't looked? How can you resist?"

"Just ain't looked yet. No point. Not till it belongs to me."

"I could never do that. I'd have to know what's in there."

Clancy snickered. "That's a woman, for ya. Gotta stick your nose in everything."

"That's right. I'll give you fifty dollars for it, just as it sits."

Clancy coughed, as if something went down the wrong pipe. "Fif—fifty? You don't even know what's in it. Could be empty."

"Will you take fifty?" I badgered.

He shoved his hands in his pockets and studied the old trunk. "Ain't really mine to sell yet. Probably wouldn't be right."

"It'll be yours tomorrow. I'll give you seventy-five."

I spotted the glimmer of a twinkle in Clancy's eye. He gazed at me with new-found admiration. I think my wheeler-dealer spirit surprised him.

"I'd be a fool to sell it, not knowing what's inside. Could be full of gold."

"Could be, but then again, like you say, could be empty; then who'd be the fool? The one who turned down cold, hard cash for a worthless trunk?"

Clancy grinned. "Fine. It's yours, if you can come up with a hundred bucks, cash. Don't want no paper-work with this one."

I stepped closer to the trunk and inspected the rusty lock. "I'll give you eighty-five. That's my top offer. What do you say?"

"Cash?"

"Cash."

"Deal."

"Great!" I pulled my wallet from my purse and sorted through the cash. "Hmm. You have change?"

"Got change in the office. Olive'll get it for you."

"Olive?"

"My wife. She takes care of the business details. She'll have change."

I followed Clancy up the dock to the run-down shack he called an office. The weather-beaten exterior hadn't seen a paintbrush in years. The faded letters on the sign over the door were barely visible. A half-dozen nets hung haphazardly from rusty nails and hooks arbitrarily placed in the walls. A cool breeze picked up the scent of sea air and decaying seaweed and carried it to my nose.

Inside, the office was not in much better condition. The green, indoor-outdoor carpet was worn through, exposing spots of wooden flooring beneath. What I could see of the walls, under dozens of posters and old photos of men standing next to big fish hanging by their tails, needed paint just as badly as the exterior.

I followed Clancy through a doorway into a smaller office. A woman sat at a desk, piled high with stacks of papers, notebooks, pencils, empty coffee cups, miscellaneous boat parts, fishing reels, and an out-of-place computer monitor, glaring a big, red warning symbol in the middle of the gray screen. Her graying hair, pulled back in a ponytail, hung longer than I'd expect for a woman her age. She had her back to us and wasn't aware of our presence. Texaco lay on a blanket next to her desk, watching her gawk at the computer screen.

"It says the application has performed an illegal function and will be shut down, Texaco. What do you suppose that means?" the woman spoke.

Texaco stared blankly at her, looking just as confused as his mistress.

"It also says that if this problem persists, I should contact the vendor. Who the heck is the vendor? We got the darn thing from a garage sale, for heaven's sake."

I smiled at the sight of a grown woman explaining her computer woes to a golden retriever.

A moment later, her tone changed, and her voice was firm. "Texaco! Did you do that? What has he been feeding you? You go outside. Oh my, that's awful. Go on! Outside!" she directed, pointing her finger at the door.

Clancy came to the dog's defense. "Come on, Olive. You know he can't help it. Don't be so hard on him."

Olive turned, surprised to see visitors in her office. "Have you been feeding him sardines again?" she demanded.

Clancy laughed and shook his head. "No, I ain't been feedin' him anything but his regular dog food. His name's Texaco cause he's got more gas than Standard Oil. You know that, Olive. Always has."

I bit my lip to keep from laughing and approached the computer monitor. "You should probably reboot," I suggested.

"Re-boot?" Olive asked.

"Yes. You know, boot it up," I explained.

"I'd like to boot it—right out the door and off the dock!" Olive complained.

"Now, come on, Olive. You know we've gotta get into the nineties, if we want to keep our business on the leading edge," Clancy reminded her.

"You mean bleeding edge, don't you? I'm ready to tear my hair out over this over-rated electronic abacus."

"Never mind that. You got some change for this little gal? I think we just need fifteen."

"Yeah, I think so. What'd she buy?" Olive pulled some bills from a cash box.

"Sold her a trunk."

She handed Clancy the cash. "Here. Let me just write up a receipt."

"No receipt," Clancy instructed.

"No receipt? Darn you, Clancy. Why do you force me to suffer with this crazy contraption so our business can be run all proper-like, then you go and do this under-the-table stuff. You're gonna make an old woman out of me!"

"You *are* an old woman, Olive."

Clancy winked and handed me the change. "There you go. It's all yours."

"Great. Give me a hand getting it off the boat?" I asked.

"Nope," Clancy replied.

At first, I thought he was kidding, but the lack of a smile on his face told me I was mistaken. "What?"

"Nope," he repeated. "You hard of hearing?"

"What if it's too heavy?" I questioned.

"I've got a bad back. Can't do any heavy lifting."

"Is there someone else around who can help?" I pleaded.

"Probably, but I don't want anyone getting hurt on *my* property. Law suits, you know."

My shoulders slumped. "Fine. Maybe it's not too heavy. I'll go check it out."

Clancy followed me back to the boat and smirked, as I climbed over the rail and attempted to pull the trunk out from under the bench. I heaved and strained to slide it a few inches.

"I'll never be able to lift this. How am I going to get it home?" I asked.

"Maybe you should open it and take it out piecemeal," he suggested.

"Okay. You have the key?"

"Don't know. There's a few keys on a ring hanging in the cabin. Maybe one of them'll open it."

"Good. Let's give it a try," I said, slightly cheerier.

Clancy stood and smiled at me, but didn't move.

I smiled back at him. "Can I have them?"

"Fifteen dollars if we find the key that works."

"Fifteen dollars!"

"Yep."

He flashed a grin at me that I'd seen all too often from overly-aggressive competitors at auctions. I pulled my wallet from my purse again.

"You're not a marine salvager; you're a pirate." I handed him the fifteen dollars.

"No, ma'am. I'm a businessman." He retrieved a ring of keys from a hook inside the cabin.

At that moment, I figured he knew exactly what was in the trunk. I bet he'd opened it the first day he brought it in. This would probably be my hundred-dollar-lesson for the day—or month.

"Thanks," I grumbled. I snatched the keys from his big, rough, weathered hand.

"Oh, now don't be mad. You probably got a real good deal," he assured me.

"I'm sure."

I tried several of the keys in the lock. Finally, I slid the right key in the rusty old lock and turned it. *Click.* I slipped the lock out of the latch and searched for a place to set it down.

Clancy held out his hand and offered to take it from me. I opened my purse and dropped it inside. "This is mine. I bought and paid for it," I reminded him.

"Just the one key. I'll want the others back."

Chapter Four

It took two trips to transfer the bright-red sea anchor, a pair of binoculars, a large ring of miscellaneous keys with a tag that read "spares," and an aluminum scuba tank to my dinghy. Clancy offered to carry the binoculars and the keys for me. I thanked him for his generous offer, but insisted on carrying everything myself. I wouldn't want him to hurt his back. He was as ornery and cantankerous as they come, but I couldn't help but like him.

I waved good-bye to Clancy, Olive, and Tex, as I motored my dinghy back to the *Plan C*. The harbor traffic had subsided considerably since my arrival this morning, and I managed to make my way, unscathed, out of Long Beach Harbor. I turned up the stereo, turned on the auto-pilot, and stretched out in a deck chair with a bottle of water and my new binoculars. I secured my big floppy sun hat with a stampede string, rubbed some SPF-30 sunscreen on my bare legs and arms, and breathed in the tropical scent of coconut. The smell reminded me of my journey through the Virgin Islands last year. I closed my eyes and recalled the warm, clear, blue waters of the Caribbean.

What a change my life took since I left my job at San Tel. A brief memory flashed through my mind—a nightmare, actually. I remember putting on my navy-blue skirt and blazer in the morning. I fussed with my makeup and hair and hurried out of the house, forgetting my lunch on the counter. When I walked through the company doors, I sensed an eerie doom. Maggie announced my arrival to a group of managers, standing outside my office. Their eyes gazed upon me like a room full of starving men, and me with only a pack of breath mints. My heart sank as I studied their faces. The database had gone down. It was costing the telecommunication company millions. I worked around the clock for days to get the thing back up. I had every tech-support person in the country on the phone, trying to figure out what was wrong. Every thirty minutes, someone from upper management called to remind me that every hour we were down cost the company a figure slightly more than I paid for my house.

I blinked my eyes and forced the memory out of my head. Everything was different now. I had changed my life; I'd left that world behind. Now, the only things I had to worry about were whether to head north, south, or west when I raised my sails, and the implication of those darn roses I put those out of my mind, too.

I changed my tune about Clancy knowing the contents of the trunk before he sold it to me. The sea anchor alone was worth at least seven or eight hundred dollars. The binoculars were also very expensive. I wasn't sure of the value of the scuba tank, but I'd been wanting to pick one up for myself, so I figured I'd keep it. All in all, I'd made a good deal.

*   *   *

The sun just kissed the surface of the Pacific as I glided into the San Diego marina slip I call home. I tied off my lines, hooked up my umbilical cord to Mother Electricity, and settled in for the night.

I picked up my cell phone and dialed Jason's number. "Hey, it's me. What're you doin'?"

"Fixing snacks for tonight's poker game," he replied, his mouth full of something the description of I probably didn't want.

"I'm afraid to ask: what are you making?" I inquired.

"Let's see. I've got nachos with extra hot jalapeño cheese, corn dogs, Cheet-o's, and potato chips. Oh, and I've got a pork-rind and pepperoni pizza in the oven—my own creation."

I cringed. "You have any idea what that kind of food is doing to your body?"

"Yeah. It makes the corners of my mouth turn up. It's called a smile; you ought to try it sometime."

"I'll stick to my fruits and vegetables, thank you very much. Hey, you up for some diving Saturday?" I asked.

"Where?"

"I was thinking we'd go out to Catalina—to the park."

"Yeah. I heard they just sunk a fifty-footer out there. Could be a fun wreck to dive."

"Great. Let's leave here about six. That too early?"

"Six is fine. Want me to pick up a tank for you? I've got to stop and have mine filled."

"No, thanks. I picked one up today in Long Beach. I'll take it down to the dive shop tomorrow and have it serviced."

"Okay. Gotta go. Someone's at the door. See you Saturday."

A vision of a pizza topped with pork rinds flashed through my head. "Only if you survive tonight's artery challenge."

"Very funny. 'Bye."

I hung up the phone, smiled, and shook my head. I could just picture the sprawl on Jason's kitchen counter: open bags of every kind of snack chip he could fit into a shopping cart; a dozen bottles of the very cheapest soda money can buy; and a great big bowl of M&M's—peanut, because, as he once explained to me, peanuts are good for you.

Jason is one of my oldest and dearest friends. I've tried to alter his eating habits, if for nothing else, to extend his life so I won't be left friendless in my old age. He tolerates my nagging, but ignores my nutrition suggestions completely. I guess it's only fair. I refuse to go on any more blind dates he tries to set me up with. His idea of my "Mr. Right" is someone who doesn't burp too loudly and can score over three million points on the pinball machine down at the Sand and Surf Bowling Alley.

Saturday's trip to Catalina was spectacular. A school of wild porpoises swam along with us for a while and thrilled me with their graceful beauty. Periodically, I'd spot a flying fish glide along the surface, then suddenly dive into the water. I remember the first time I'd ever seen a flying fish: I thought it was a bird. I worried when it dove in the water and didn't resurface. When I saw three more do the same thing, I thought they must be the stupidest birds in the world.

The state park, off of Catalina Island, offers a popular spot for diving. The area is protected, so the sea life tend to be more sociable than usual. There are several wrecks to add interest to the dives.

I dropped the sails. "This looks like a good spot."

"I'll get the anchor," Jason offered. "You're sort of quiet today. What's up?"

"Oh, nothing." I shrugged.

"Come on. Don't give me that 'Oh, nothing' business. I've known you too long. Something's eating at you," he pestered.

"Well, there might be something on my mind. You probably don't want to hear about it."

He shrugged his shoulders and jumped up from his seat. "Okay. Let's gear up, then."

"What? You're giving up, just like that?" I whined.

"If you don't want to talk about it, I don't want to pressure you."

"I didn't say I don't want to talk about it. I said you probably don't want to hear about it. I *want* to talk about it. I *need* to talk about it."

Jason sat back down. "Then talk, girl. I'm all ears."

"It's about Craig."

"You're right. I don't want to hear about it."

"Jason! Please. This is important."

"Okay. I'm sorry. Go ahead. Where is the ol' Craig-meister, anyway?"

"He's in New York for a few days—a medical convention."

"So, what's the problem?"

"Did you see those roses on my table?"

"Yeah. From him?"

"Yeah. Here, read the note." I handed him the card that came with the flower delivery.

Jason pulled the small, delicate card from the envelope and opened it. "Marry me? He wants to get married?"

"Yes. Oh, Jason. What am I gonna do?"

"You're asking me? I'm not sure I see the problem here. I thought you were crazy about this guy."

"I am. But marriage? What if it doesn't work out? What if he wants me to change? What if—"

"What if a meteor hits the earth tomorrow, and we all burn up in a puff of smoke?"

I snatched the card back from him. "What should I do?"

"Oh, no. I'm not going there. This is your deal, Dev. If I tell you to marry him, and he turns out to be a jerk, then I'll be the scum who gave you bad advice. If I tell you to blow him off, then you'll always wonder what might have been. You can't honestly expect me to tell you what to do, can you?"

"No. You're right. I just needed to talk to someone about it. I'm so darn independent, you know. I just don't know if I can deal with the commitment and the compromises. My life is so simple right now. I don't want to mess it up."

"You'll make the right decision. You always land on your feet. Now, let's get to the more important matter of the day. You ready?"

We suited up. Jason helped me on with my tank.

"Where'd you say you picked this up?" he asked.

"It was in a trunk I bought, over in Long Beach. I had Paddy's Dive Shop top it off. It's full."

"Good. Hey, what'd you bring for lunch?"

"We'll have a nice green salad with a raspberry vinaigrette and soy burgers. You'll like it."

"What? No hotdogs?"

"Oh, yeah. I've got tofu-dogs. You want those instead?"

"Jeez! I knew I should've brought leftover pizza."

I smirked at him and stuffed his mouthpiece in his face. "Just be quiet, Jason Walters, or there'll be no food for you at all!"

I adjusted the mouthpiece between my lips, pulled my mask down over my face, and jumped into the warm Pacific water. Jason followed my lead.

Five minutes into the dive, I began to feel lightheaded. I wondered if the thought of Jason's pork-rind pizza had gotten the better of me. I felt a little queasy. I stopped and touched Jason on the shoulder. He looked at me, questioning. I held my hand to my stomach, then to my head. He shrugged his shoulders and held his arms out, not understanding my signals. I pointed up to the surface with my thumb and began ascending. I figured he would either follow or not, but I had to get to the surface before I passed out.

Luckily, we weren't very deep. As soon as my head bobbed out of the water, I spit out my mouthpiece and gasped for fresh air. Confused, I frantically searched for the *Plan C*. Jason surfaced seconds later, a few feet away.

"What's the matter? You okay?" he asked.

"No. I think I'm sick. Came on really sudden."

"Can you make it to the boat?"

"I think so. Where is it?"

"Over here. Come on."

Jason helped me up the ladder and onto the deck. I

dropped the heavy tank off my back and collapsed in a cushioned deck chair. Jason rushed to the galley and brought me a bottle of water.

"Here. Feel any better?" he asked, handing me the water.

"A little. I can't figure what brought it on. I felt fine when we started out."

Jason eyed the bright-yellow scuba tank I'd dropped haphazardly on the deck. "You say you had Paddy's fill that tank?"

"Yeah. Why?" I replied.

"I don't know. Paddy runs a good dive shop. He's always careful. We ought to have it checked out."

Paddy turned the valve and smelled the air coming out of the tank. "Smells okay," he reported. "But then, carbon monoxide is odorless."

"Carbon monoxide?" I questioned.

"Leading cause of accidental poisoning death in the country." Paddy went to a drawer and pulled a disk-shaped device out. "This is a carbon monoxide detector. I'll bet that's what it is."

"But how would it get in the tank?" I asked.

"Well, it didn't come from here. We run a clean shop. Tank was half full when you brought it in. Could be some genius filled it at a gas station or in his garage with a gasoline-powered air compressor. Seen it happen before. You're lucky to be alive."

I jumped when the loud beeping alarm on the detector blared, indicating a dangerous level of the poisonous gas escaping from the scuba tank. A shiver ran up my spine as my eyes met Jason's.

Chapter Five

Olive answered the phone as professionally as I'm sure Clancy insisted. "Tex and Clancy's Marine Salvage. You sink it; we save it."

"Good morning, Olive. This is Devonie Lace. I bought a trunk from your husband last week. Remember me?"

"Oh, yes. You're the little girl who helped me with the computer problem I was having. Everything alright?"

I smiled at the memory of Olive, soliciting technical computer advice from Tex, the dog.

"To be honest, no. I wonder if you were ever contacted by the owner of the *Little Maria?*"

"No, not a word. Why?"

"That scuba tank, from the trunk I bought, was full of carbon monoxide. Made me really sick. I'm concerned that maybe the owner of the boat may have had more tanks contaminated with it."

"Oh, my stars! Carbon monoxide? Are you kidding?" Olive gasped.

"No. I think your husband better have the other tanks from that boat checked out."

"I'll have someone come check them right away. Are you okay?"

38

"I'm fine. I was lucky," I said.

I could hear Clancy in the background, pestering his wife. "Do I have to call a lawyer? Is she gonna sue us?"

Olive shushed her husband. She must have placed her hand over the receiver, because her next sentence was muffled. All I could make out were the words, ". . . you old fool." Then, she came back on the line.

"You're not going to sue us, are you?" she asked.

"Of course not," I assured her. "This is a buyer-beware business. I should have had the tank emptied and tested before I ever used it."

"I'm just glad you're okay. Thanks for the warning. We don't want anyone else to get a hold of one of those tanks before we check them out."

I pulled a pen from a small glass jar on my galley table. "I wonder if you would give me the name of the previous owner of the *Little Maria?* You must have been able to get that information from the registration records."

Olive shuffled through some papers. "Let's see. What was his name? I have it here, somewhere. Oh, yes. Here it is. Hastings. Roy Hastings. Lives over in Avalon. We tried to contact him, but he never responded."

"Roy Hastings?" I wrote it down on a small notepad.

"That's right. Funny. Some fellow came by yesterday, asking about the boat. Wondered if anyone ever showed up to claim it. He was real curious about the stuff on the boat."

"Really? Did you get his name?" I asked.

"No. Didn't leave his name."

"Did he say what his business was with the boat?"

"No. Just curious, like you. Wanted to know if everything was just the way we found it. I told him yes, except, of course, for the trunk we sold you. He hung around for a bit, then left. Like I said, nice fellow."

I dropped the pen back in its glass jar. "Thanks, Olive. You've been a big help."

I took a bite out of a Fuji apple and chewed it while I waited for Spencer to answer his phone.

"Hello?" came the voice through the telephone.

I hesitated, still chewing my mouthful of apple. Finally, I got the words out. "Spencer. It's Devonie."

"Devonie? That name sounds familiar. I used to have a friend named Devonie, but she took off for the Caribbean last year, and I haven't seen or heard from her since. Not even a postcard."

"It's good to hear your voice, Spence. I'm back from the Caribbean, and I need your help."

"Of course you do. I was just sitting here, waiting for your call. That's my new job description, you know: Information Technology Expert to Devonie Lace."

"I'm glad to see you haven't changed. You still with the State?" I asked.

"You kidding? Cushiest job I ever had. I'm working over at the DOJ. Been there since Christmas."

"DOJ?"

"Yeah. Department of Justice—rap sheets, firearm permits, dactylograms."

"Dactylo-whats?"

"Dactylograms. You know, fingerprints. Where'd you go to school?"

"Same place you did. Guess I missed the day they taught us that one. Seriously, though, can you check on a name for me? Roy Hastings, from Avalon, California. It's kind of important, and you know I wouldn't ask if—"

"Not to worry. This is your good buddy, Spencer, you're talking to. What'd this guy do? Write your name on the restroom wall at the Bar & Grille? Stand you up for a date? Put that terrible picture of you out on the Internet?"

"My home page? Are you the one who—"

"Oops. I swear, I didn't have anything to do with it."

"Spencer! I should have known it was you. You owe me, big time!"

"Okay, okay. What's this guy's name? Ray?"

"No. Roy. Roy Hastings."

"Got anything else? A driver's license number? A social-security number? Anything?"

"No. Sorry. Do your best. I'm not expecting miracles."

"Good thing, 'cause you're not gonna get one."

"Aw, come on, Spence. You're underestimating yourself. Remember, you're the *King of Hackers*. You pull off miracles all the time."

"Flattery will get you everywhere. I'll see what I can do. I'll give you a call, when I find something."

"Thanks, Spence."

I knocked on Jason's door and waited. I could hear him inside, banging around in the kitchen.

"Open up! It's the food police! We've had a report of criminal nutrition activity going on at this address!" I hollered.

He opened the door. A string of melted cheese hung off his lip and stuck to his chin. He held the smoking gun: a huge slice of pepperoni pizza, with an additional topping I couldn't immediately identify.

"Dev. Hi. Come on in." He opened the door and let me in. "Want some pizza? It's my latest creation—pepperoni, sausage and butterscotch chip. Sort of dinner and dessert, all in one."

I crinkled my nose at his offering. "My God, Jason. I'm gonna refer you to a good cardiologist. Maybe he can talk some sense into you."

I sat down at the cluttered kitchen table and pushed aside moved a package of Oreo cookies, an empty bag of fries, and a half-full can of diet soda.

"Hey, want to catch a movie? That new one I've been wanting to see just opened," I asked.

"The chick flick?" he shot back.

"It's not a chick flick. It's a romantic comedy."

"Alright. But next time, we're going to see something with nothing but car chases, shootouts, foul language, and explosions. And don't ask for any more advice about Craig. I'm not in that business. Deal?"

"Fine. Let's go."

"Okay. I just have to feed the neighbor's dog first. They're on vacation for three weeks. Come on. You can help."

It was late by the time I got back to the *Plan C*. I fumbled with the keys and finally found the right one for the hatch door. Something didn't seem right when

I grabbed the handle. The door wasn't locked. *I know I locked it,* I thought to myself. I cautiously opened the door, and reached around the corner to turn on the light. My heart sank when I gazed at the sight.

Utensils thrown on the floor. Clothes tossed everywhere. Drawers wide open, empty. The contents of every cupboard, closet, and drawer were strewn all over the carpet. My beautiful boat had been violated.

It suddenly occurred to me that the culprit may still be onboard. My heart began to pound and my knees grew weak. I felt my face flush and perspiration form on my forehead. I tiptoed to my cabin and retrieved the baseball bat I keep next to my bed. Poised, ready to clobber anyone who might still be onboard, I slowly crept through the galley into the main salon, peered into all the guest cabins and heads, then back to the master bedroom. I hoisted the hatch door up and shone my flashlight down below, watching for any movement at all. Whoever made this mess was long gone.

I returned to the living room, slumped my tired body in a chair, and rested my chin on the butt of the baseball bat. I let my disappointed eyes gaze around the mess made by some low-life, worthless trash who certainly didn't deserve to live, and thought of at least eight forms of torture I'd like to inflict on the little weasel.

After the police report had been filed and the officers left, I started the cleanup process. Exhausted, but determined to take a full inventory before I went to bed, it took me three hours to put everything back together. I laid my head on my folded arms, while I sat at the galley table. As far as I could tell, there was nothing missing.

Chapter Six

Olive had her back to the door and the phone stuck to her ear when I walked in. She was staring, mesmerized, at the image of sheets of paper flying across her computer screen, leaving one folder and placing themselves neatly into another. Texaco sat faithfully at his mistress's feet, watching her, intently, with his big, brown eyes.

I opened my mouth to announce my presence, but was interrupted by Olive's frustrated voice barking into the telephone. "No! Don't put me on hold again. I've been on hold for—shoot!"

In disgust, she held the phone out in front of Tex's face. "They put me on hold again, Tex. I've been on hold for over twenty minutes. All I want to know is why this stupid machine told me, over an hour ago, that there was only fifteen minutes remaining for it to do whatever the heck it was doing. Five minutes ago, it said there was ten minutes remaining, and now, it says there's thirteen! It's making me crazy, Tex! Crazy!"

I walked around to the other side of the desk and set my purse in a chair.

"Oh. Hello, Devonie. I didn't hear you come in."

Olive jammed the phone back in its usual position between her left ear and shoulder.

"On the line with technical support?" I whispered.

"Technical support? You kidding? I don't think the three kids I've spoken to in the last half-hour know how to operate a telephone, let alone a computer. The only buttons they seem to be familiar with are 'hold' and 'transfer.' "

I smiled. "Why don't you hang up? Maybe I can help."

You'd have thought I'd removed the earth from her shoulders. She quickly placed the receiver in its cradle and stood up, ready for me to take the pilot seat.

I think the information revolution, with the introduction of computers into the lives of nearly every person in the free world, must be a lot like the introduction of automobiles to a society accustomed to warm-blooded, four-legged, hay-eating horses. Horses, for the most part, were reliable and predictable. When old Bessie was off her feed, nearly everyone in town could tell you what was wrong with her and how to cure her, if you didn't already know, yourself. But, be the first one on your block with one of those newfangled Fords, and try to find *anyone* within a hundred miles to explain why it won't start. I wonder how many years it took to get a population of knowledgeable mechanics planted everywhere they were needed?

With a few keystrokes and some well-placed mouse-clicks, I'd resolved Olive's computer dilemma.

"God bless you, Devonie," Olive gushed, as I surrendered her chair back to her. "You're a genius."

"I'm not a genius. I've just been there before." I've lost count of how many times I've been proclaimed a genius for performing some small task that seemed like nothing to me, but meant the world to the person trying to accomplish it. There are plenty of gurus out there much more computer savvy than I am, but I do get a kick out of helping people through their computer woes. Makes me feel a little like the Lone Ranger.

Clancy stepped into the office, accompanied by a man. The man was tall, about forty, with dark, wavy hair and a mustache. His plaid shirt was neatly pressed, and he carried a leather briefcase. Clancy stopped short when he saw me sitting opposite Olive. "Oh, jeez! Do I have to call a lawyer? You change your mind about suing us?"

Olive turned and swatted him with a ruler. "Hush up, you old fool!"

I laughed and shook my head. "No, I'm not going to sue you. But I could use your help."

"Help? What do I look like? The pope?" Clancy replied, with more than a hint of sarcasm.

Olive hit him again, this time with feeling. "Clancy McGreggor! If you don't knock it off, you'll be sleeping with Tex tonight!"

"Good. Least he doesn't snore. Be the best night sleep I've had since I married you."

Olive slapped the ruler down on the desk. "You sorry old coot!"

Clancy sauntered up behind Olive and gave her a kiss on the cheek. "I'm just kidding, darlin'. You know I love ya more than that old dog."

Clancy looked me over from head to toe. "You don't look no worse for wear. What sort of help you looking for?"

I retrieved a large ring of keys from my purse. "These are the keys from that trunk you sold me. I'd like see if I can find something one of them might fit."

"Don't believe I ever met anyone as nosy as you."

I glared at Clancy. "Last night, someone broke into my boat. They tore the place apart looking for something. They didn't take anything."

Clancy scratched his whiskery face and adjusted the cap on his head. "And that means what?"

"I don't know," I admitted. "There're just a lot of weird things going on about that boat. First of all, it's abandoned. You have to admit that's strange. Then, the poisoned scuba tank. Next, a stranger comes by to inquire about the *Little Maria*, and you tell him about me buying the trunk. Coincidentally, my boat gets ransacked, but nothing is taken. I'd like to know what it's all about; I'd like to take a look at the *Little Maria,* again."

"Look all you want. Don't know what you think you're gonna find, though. Sounds like what you really need is a good insurance agent. This here's Morgan—best in the business." Clancy motioned to the man who came in with him.

The man held out his hand. "Morgan Johnson, West Coast Insurance."

I shook his hand and forced a cordial smile. I didn't need any more insurance salesmen trying to convince me I'm on the verge of economic disaster. I've decided that the whole insurance concept may not be such a good idea. Your money suddenly belongs to the insurance company, and the last thing they want to do is give it back when it's needed. And the insurance companies still keep asking for more money, without giving any more services in exchange.

"Actually, I'm not an agent. I'm an investigator. I specialize in marine losses. Most of my work takes place underwater, but our company does handle property damage, robbery, and vandalism cases. Do you currently have a policy?" he inquired.

"I'm covered, thanks. So, you must do a lot of diving in your line of work."

"I do, as a matter of fact. I heard Clancy had a bunch of scuba tanks he might want to part with. Thought I'd come take a look."

Clancy and Morgan followed me over the rail of the *Little Maria.* There was storage under the bench seating. I found a key that released the padlock and lifted the benches, revealing dozens of life jackets.

"I'll let you buy this key back from me," I said, smiling, as I held the key out to Clancy.

"Don't need it—not now that you've opened it."

"Okay. I'll keep it then." I replaced the padlock and snapped it closed.

"Hey! Wait a minute. Open that back up," he barked.

"Don't need to—not now that I've seen what's in there," I said with a grin.

Clancy frowned and folded his arms across his big chest. "How much?"

I scratched my head. "Seems to me you put a value of fifteen dollars on a key that gains access to an unknown end. This one ought to be worth at least twenty."

"Twenty! You gotta be out of your mind!" Clancy barked.

I dropped the key in my purse and stood up.

Clancy's hands fell to his sides and his shoulders slumped in defeat. "Fine. Twenty dollars. Who's the pirate?" Clancy complained.

"Hey. I learned from the best," I reminded him.

Clancy dug a wadded-up bill from his pocket and, reluctantly, placed it in my hand.

My search turned up four fire extinguishers, one first-aid kit, two dozen flares, and a twenty-man survival raft. Below deck, I counted fifty dive tanks and an equal number of weight belts.

"Had every one of those tanks checked," Clancy assured me. "Not a whiff of carbon monoxide."

"Good," I replied.

Morgan stayed below to check out the tanks. Clancy followed me back to the bridge. I studied the GPS monitor mounted on the panel. "Isn't that a Global Positioning System?" I asked.

"Yeah. Darn nice one, too. Been thinking of taking it off her and using it on my boat," Clancy replied.

"I bet this one stores a bunch of locations. Have you checked it out?"

"Not yet."

"Mind if I turn it on?"

"Go ahead," he allowed.

I powered the device up and stared at the green screen. "How does it work?" I questioned.

Clancy sidled up to the apparatus and started pressing buttons. "Here. You just press this one to recall your stored locations. If you press that one, it shows them with the date and time. See?"

I watched as dozens of lines of cryptic codes scrol-

Gina Cresse

led up the screen. "Slow down. Can we sort this by date and time? Descending?"

"Heck, probably. Let's see. I think if I just push this one . . . Oops, that's not right. Wait. . . ." He fumbled with the buttons.

I worried that he may erase something important. "That's okay. Lets not try anything too spectacular. How about if we just scroll down to the end. Maybe they're already in order."

"I know I can do it, if you just let me—"

"Really. I think they're already sorted. Look."

Clancy stared at the screen. "Hmm. . . . Guess you're right."

He scrolled down to the last entry stored. The date, time, longitude, latitude, and an alphanumeric identifier displayed at the bottom of the list. I enunciated the words, " '*El Niño* wreck.' Look at the date. November tenth. Isn't that about the time you found the abandoned boat?"

Clancy scratched his head. "Yeah. I think so. About a week later."

I looked at my watch, then gazed out over the horizon. "Think your friend, Morgan, would be up for a dive this morning?"

It took us a little more than two hours to get to the position identified on the GPS. Clancy cut the engine and dropped the anchor. "Well. This is it," he announced.

Morgan checked the reading on the depth indicator. "Hundred and fifty feet. You ever go down that far, Devonie?"

"No. Deepest I've ever gone down is fifty feet," I admitted.

"You sure you want to do this? Going down one-fifty poses certain risks," Morgan warned.

"Risks?" My voice wavered a little.

"Nitrogen narcosis. Affects your ability to think and make judgments. Basically, breathing air at a pressure of four or more atmospheres can turn you into a falling-down drunk," Morgan explained.

"What else?" I asked.

Morgan crossed his arms on his chest. "Well, then there's oxygen poisoning. What we're breathing right now is about seventy-eight percent nitrogen and twenty-one percent oxygen. Excess oxygen can damage lung tissue and adversely affect the central nervous system. Oxygen poisoning can occur when the partial pressure of pure oxygen equals two atmospheres absolute."

Clancy gaped as his friend spieled off gas ratios and PSI figures. Finally, he added his two-cents worth. "And don't forget the bends."

Morgan stopped and smiled at Clancy. "That's right. There's always the risk of the bends. You ever get the bends, Clancy?"

Clancy bent over and held his hand to his back. "Every morning, when I get out of bed."

We all laughed. I stood up and grabbed a tank. "Okay, I've heard the risks. I'm ready. Let's do it."

Morgan stayed close as we descended. He continually checked to make sure I felt okay. As we approached the sea floor, the powerful light beam from his flashlight shone on something white—big and white. We swam to the rail. She was huge. A hundred feet, I guessed. We glided along her side and inspected her all around. A mural painted on the port side depicted a school of dolphins playing in the surf. On the starboard side, a similar mural immortalized a pair of orcas, one diving and one breaching. As we rounded the last curve, I read the name painted on the stern: *Gigabyte.*

Morgan touched me on the shoulder and pointed to his watch. Our ten minutes were up; we had to return to the surface.

Clancy helped me over the railing, then reached for Morgan's hand. I struggled to get my gear off.

Morgan climbed over the rail, spat out his mouthpiece, and ranted, "Do you know what that is down there? My God! That's the *Gigabyte!*"

"Bates's yacht?" Clancy asked.

"Bates's yacht! Yes! She's down there, right now! The whole country's been looking for that yacht for six months and we've found it! Where's my phone? I've gotta call the office," Morgan babbled.

"Well, I'll be danged. What do you think the salvage award would be on that one?" Clancy asked.

"Salvage? Clancy, it's a hundred-footer. It'll take a couple barges to bring her up. You don't have the equipment to raise something that size. I'll call the Coast Guard."

"Now, wait a minute, Morgan. Maybe I can get my hands on—"

"Clancy." Morgan held up a halting hand. "This is Gerald Bates's yacht we're talking about. The man is the richest computer industrialist in the world. He and this yacht have been missing for over six months. You think the Bates Corporation is going to let Tex and Clancy's Marine Salvage get anywhere within a mile of this spot when they find out?"

I watched Clancy's chin drop two floors. He knew Morgan was right.

"Olive and me could retire on what that salvage award would be."

Morgan put an arm over Clancy's shoulders. "Retire? You? Then how would you have any fun? You can't ever retire, old man. You wouldn't know what to do with yourself with no purpose in life."

"Maybe so. But I sure as heck wouldn't mind giving it a try for a while," Clancy pouted.

"I know, Clancy. But, you know I'm right, don't you?"

"I suppose. Go ahead. Make the call."

I sat quietly on a padded bench and gazed at the two men arguing about the salvage award, but didn't see or hear them at all. My mind was a thousand miles away. We had just discovered Gerald Bates's sunken yacht. Gerald Bates, the wealthiest man in the world.

Chapter Seven

I banged on Spencer's door for the third time. "Come on, Spence. Open up!" I yelled into the solid piece of oak standing between me and the most accomplished computer geek this side of the Mississippi—and probably the other side, for that matter. I could hear his pathetic voice call back to me from somewhere inside the house.

During the twelve-hour drive from San Diego to Sacramento, I tried to imagine what Spencer's house might look like. I pictured a scene from NASA: rows of computer terminals; little orange, red, and green flashing lights; racks full of electronic paraphernalia; wires running along the baseboards, anchored with straps and ties, disappearing into countless boxes mounted on the walls. You'd have to know Spencer to understand why I'd conjure up such a picture.

"Devonie? Is that you?" I could hear him fumble with the lock. The door opened slowly, and a picture I didn't expect brought a smile to my face.

I'd driven all night; it was nearly six in the morning by the time I arrived in Sacramento. I'd obviously gotten Spencer out of bed. His mouth opened in a yawn so large, I could see his tonsils. He scratched his head and rubbed his eyes. His hair, naturally brown, but

54

bleached to a nearly yellow blond, stood straight up from his head. Too much bleaching and styling gel left the mess looking like the victim of a lightning strike. He stood about six-foot-four and probably weighed about one-seventy, soaking wet. The skinny frame was bare from the waist up. I'd never seen Spencer without a shirt before; my eyes fixed on a small tattoo permanently branded onto his chest. The image, a green square with small black and silver dots and lines running in all directions like a city street map, was framed with the words, "I love my Motherboard." From the waist down, an entirely different story was told. On his slim hips, Spiderman pajama pants hung too short for his long legs—the hem fell about mid-calf. His bare feet were large and striking against the tile floor. I gawked at the curled up toes on those number twelves. "You paint your toenails?" I marveled.

He glanced down at the bright-red tips on his toes and wiggled them proudly. "Like them? Cindy did it. She's practicing to get her cosmetology license. I could find out the color for you, if you want."

"That's okay. I go for a lighter shade," I replied, grinning.

I picked up the heavy scuba tank I'd brought and carried it inside. I set it down in the entryway and marveled at the surroundings—not a computer in sight. Nothing on the walls but tasteful artwork and bookshelves. The only electronics I could see were the usual: television, stereo, VCR, and microwave oven. I set my purse on the table. "Is this your parents' house?"

"No. Why?"

"Oh, I don't know. I just pictured something different."

Spencer examined the scuba tank. "This the tank you want to check out?" he asked.

"Yeah. Think we can lift any prints off it?"

"Don't know. It's been in the water. You've been handling it like a stress ball. Probably been touched by a half-dozen people since you bought it. What's the deal with it, anyway?"

"You seen the news today?" I asked.

"News?"

I picked up the remote and turned on the television. Nearly every station has reporting the discovery of Gerald Bates's yacht, the *Gigabyte.*

Spencer sat down in a big, leather recliner and gaped at the TV screen. "They found Bates?"

"No, not Bates. Just his yacht. Actually, I found it."

"You? How?"

"The guy who owned this tank, and the boat I got it from, discovered the wreck and recorded its location on his GPS. That's Roy Hastings, the guy I asked you to check out. Get anything?"

"Not much. Nothing on him in the California Criminal History database. I went to the DMV database. Got the basics: date of birth, height, weight, address. Had a pickup and a boat registered in his name and a certified dive instructor license issued back in the seventies."

"That's it? Nothing else?" I said, disappointed.

"That's all I could come up with. If you want to know more, why don't you call the guy up and ask him yourself?"

"I would, if he were anywhere on the face of the

Earth. It seems the *Gigabyte* was Hastings's last stop before he disappeared. This tank, complete with poison gas, was on Hastings's boat when it was found, abandoned."

Spencer scratched his mop-top head and peered at the tank. "Just let me down some Cheerios and grab a quick shower; then, we can run it down to the DOJ."

Spencer had commandeered a small Radio Flyer wagon from his garage to transport the tank. I don't know why a grown man with no children has a little wagon, but then, I don't know why he allowed his girlfriend to paint his toenails, either.

I pulled the wagon through the massive glass doors Spencer held open for me. A guard behind a glass wall glanced up from his morning paper.

"Morning, Spencer. Kind of early for you, isn't it?"

"Special project. Research knows no time boundaries," Spencer replied. "Hey, Howard. This is Devonie Lace. I need a guest badge for her."

"Sure thing. Just fill out this form." Howard pushed a sheet of paper and pen under the pass-through.

Howard issued me a special guest badge and let us through the glass doors into the California Department of Justice building. I pulled the little wagon behind me down the long corridors, following Spencer through the maze of hallways.

A man trudged from the other direction, overburdened with a stack of folders. He stopped to rest and propped his load on a handrail. "Morning, Spencer."

"Good morning, Marv," Spencer replied. "How's it going?"

Marv rolled his eyes and adjusted his grip on the mass of paper in his arms. "It's going to be one of *those* days. I can just tell."

"What's the problem?" Spencer pried.

"You name it. I've got fifty-two apps for gun permits, here: four of 'em ex-postal workers, eighteen recently divorced, nine with rap sheets a mile long. Man, they've got nerve. To top it all off, Hollywood wants to blow up the city of San Francisco, and the joker who filed the app, thinks it'll be more *artistic* if they do it for real, instead of hiring the special effects team."

Spencer chuckled and patted the weary man on the back. "Cheer up, Marv. Only fifteen more years till retirement."

"Thanks a lot, Spencer," Marv grumbled, and then he continued on his long trek down the hallway and disappeared around a corner.

We pushed through a pair of swinging doors and entered some sort of lab. A man sat on a stool in front of a strange-looking device and peered over his glasses at us. Then he glanced at my little wagon. "Sorry, guys. I can't come out and play right now. I've got work to do."

"Everyone's a comedian. Hey, Sam, this is Devonie." Spencer motioned toward me and I extended my hand. "We want to lift some prints off this tank. Any ideas?" Spencer continued.

Sam examined the tank, reclined in the wagon. "Hmm. Been in the water?"

"Yes," I admitted.

Sam shook his head. "How old are the prints you want to lift?"

"I don't know. Probably at least six months," I replied.

Sam frowned, his head still shaking. "Six months ... been submerged. Hope you're not hanging your hat on these prints."

Spencer kneeled next to the wagon. "To top it off, it's been handled by every Tom, Dick, and Harry this side of the border. We'll be lucky to get one good print."

Sam took the handle of the wagon and pulled it to the end of a long bench. "Don't think superglue will work. Best bet is probably the VMD."

"VMD?" I questioned.

"VMD. That's Vacuum Metal Deposition," Sam explained.

I raised an eyebrow and looked at Spencer, waiting for more information. Spencer shrugged his shoulders. "You got me. By the time I get them, they've already been developed and are ready to load into the computer."

Sam put on a pair of latex rubber gloves and hoisted the tank up onto the bench. "VMD develops latent prints in situations where other methods fail."

"How does it work?" I asked.

"Well, we just put the tank in this sealed chamber," Sam explained as he closed the door on the box. "Then all the air is sucked out, making it a vacuum. A few milligrams of gold and zinc are evaporated in the chamber. The gold and zinc interact with the stuff that makes up a fingerprint. The metals will condense on the tank, rendering usable images out of any latent prints. Pretty remarkable."

"How long does it take?" I further questioned.

"About fifteen minutes. Enough time to go have a coffee break. Come on," he motioned. "Just put on a fresh pot."

We found fourteen usable prints on the tank. Usable, in that there was enough of the fingerprint pattern area to make a comparison and, hopefully, an identification. Spencer loaded the developed fingerprint images into a computer, and we began the process of separating and grouping them. After that procedure, we determined fourteen prints belonging to a total of five different fingers—fingers from people, as yet, unidentified.

Spencer stood and walked to a machine labeled, "Live Scan." "Come over here," he called to me.

I obeyed and stood next to the contraption, gazing at the glass plate.

"Put your hand on the glass," he instructed.

I looked at Spencer and hid my hands behind my back.

"It's okay; won't hurt. Promise. This is Live Scan. We use it to scan fingerprints directly to a file. We'll scan yours, then eliminate them from the database to narrow our search."

"I see." I placed my hand on the glass and waited while the machine made the equivalent of a Xerox copy of my handprint.

We sat down at the computer and Spencer brought an image of a fingerprint up on the screen. "Okay. Let's see what kind of score this one gets."

I watched, mesmerized by the technology.

"Six-fifty. No match. Let's try the next one." He brought up the next print and retried the operation.

"Bingo. Thirty-eight-ninety-two. That's you."

"How can you tell?" I asked.

"Got a score over three thousand. Anything over a thousand is a possible. Anything over three thousand is a pretty definite match."

"Wow. Now what?"

"Now, we see if we can find a hit with the other four fingers we got. Tell me who you know for sure has handled it besides you," Spencer asked.

"Let's see. Jason helped me with it. Paddy, down at the dive shop—he filled it and checked it for me. And Clancy—no, wait—Clancy didn't touch it; he made me carry the heavy stuff. Real gentleman. That's it."

Spencer rubbed his chin with the back of his hand. "Not likely we'll find a match in this database, unless they've been arrested. But I have access to some others we can search. Maybe we'll get lucky."

Hours of searching through millions of records turned up nothing. Exhausted from driving all night, I laid my head on my folded arms on the desk. "I guess this was a mistake. I'm sorry I wasted your time, Spencer."

Spencer patted the back of my head. "You're not throwing in the towel, are you? That's not the Devonie I know. What happened to that tenacious, strong-willed, hardheaded, never-give-up-till-you're-dead girl?"

"She fell asleep two hours ago," I moaned.

Spencer ignored my whining and continued searching the database. I closed my eyes and was about to drift off into a light sleep, when Spencer's excited voice startled me out of my tired misery. "Bingo! We got a hit!"

I raised my head and stared at the computer screen. I blinked my eyes a few times to focus on the small, green characters. "Kent Morrison? Who the heck is he?"

"Kent Morrison. Retired. U.S. Naval Intelligence. Here, I'll print it out."

My glassy eyes stared blankly at the printout Spencer handed me. I couldn't think. A good night's sleep and another twelve-hour drive back to San Diego would give me time to think about what I'd discovered and decide what to do next.

Chapter Eight

Spencer waved as I backed out of his driveway and aimed my Jeep down the quiet street of the old neighborhood.

By the time I got to Bakersfield, my stomach was growling nonstop—reminding me I hadn't eaten for six hours. I pulled off the highway and found a place that looked like it might have a decent salad bar.

As I picked through the broccoli florets on my plate, I gazed out the big glass window toward the parking lot. A black-and-white police car pulled into the lot and parked across from my Jeep. I set my fork down and watched as the two officers sat in their car, talking; then one spoke into the radio.

I finished my salad and paid my bill, then pushed through the glass doors and headed for my Jeep. As I slid the key into the door lock, the state troopers got out of their squad car and approached me. The driver was tall and muscular. The brown hair I could see from under his cap was cut very short. With one, big, continuous eyebrow that covered both eyes, he looked an awful lot like a character I'd seen on the professional wrestling circuit. The brass nameplate pinned to his uniform said his name was Henry Vladowski. His partner was slightly shorter and about ten years older. For some reason, he had no nameplate to identify him. He stayed one step behind Vladowski and kept both eyes fixed on me.

I smiled. "Afternoon."

Neither one returned a smile. No friendly greeting at all. Officer Vladowski had his hand on his gun. "This your vehicle?"

"Yes. Why?" I questioned.

"Put your hands on the hood," Vladowski ordered.

"What?"

"Put your hands on the hood now!" he yelled again.

A small crowd had gathered in the doorway of the restaurant and watched the two peace officers in action. I obeyed their orders, placing my trembling hands on the hood of my Jeep. I could feel the pace of my heart speed up. My legs felt weak, and I leaned on the Jeep to keep from falling. Dozens of eyes stared at me like I was some sort of criminal. People in passing cars slowed down to gawk at the sight. I wanted to slide under the Jeep and disappear.

"What's this all about? There must be some sort of mistake," I insisted, my voice trembling. The shorter officer frisked me from head to toe in search of a weapon.

"This vehicle was reported stolen this morning. You fit the description of the perpetrator. You have any ID?" Vladowski asked.

I couldn't have heard him correctly. My heart was pounding so hard, I could hear it beating in my ears. "Stolen? It's not stolen. This is *my* Jeep. My driver's license is in my purse, and the registration's in the glove box."

The unidentified officer took my keys, while Vladowski searched through my purse for my wallet. He opened it up to my license. "Are you Devonie Lace?"

"Yes, that's me, and this Jeep is registered to me."

"Not according to the DMV. Belongs to Mr. and Mrs. Ryan Hayes. You stole it from them at gunpoint this morning in front of their home. Recall that?" Vladowski accused.

I shook my head to clear the pounding that was going on in my ears. I felt as though I might pass out at any minute. I worked to control my breathing, so I wouldn't hyperventilate. "That's ridiculous. You've got the wrong person."

Vladowski's partner removed the registration certificate from the glove box and closed the passenger-side door. "Take a look at this, Hank."

The officers inspected the registration certificate that identified me as the owner of the vehicle. Vladowski took the certificate to his patrol car and got on the radio, while his partner kept an eye on me. The crowd of onlookers grew into a small mob.

When Vladowski returned, he took me by the arm and led me to the patrol car. "We have to go down to the station."

I closed my eyes and took a deep breath, trying to keep my composure. "So, am I under arrest?"

"Not yet. There're some discrepancies here we need to straighten out. According to the DMV computer, you're not the registered owner of this vehicle."

For some reason, as soon as he mentioned the word, "computer," I felt a slight sense of relief. "Great— another computer foul-up," I grumbled under my breath. Vladowski shoved me, head first, into the black-and-white limo that would transport me to a place I knew I didn't want to go.

Five-and-a-half hours later, officer Vladowski and his partner, who I'd come to think of as *The Shadow,* offered me their deepest regret and apologized for the unfortunate foul-up with the computer system.

"Oh, that's okay. It's straightened out now." I gathered up my purse and got to my feet. Did I just tell them it's okay that they detained me for nearly six hours? And did I say it with a smile, as though I enjoyed the entire, humiliating experience? Am I an idiot? Maybe I should plaster a sign on my back that says, "Kick me—and have a nice day."

By the time I found my Jeep, a team of men in dark blue coveralls were replacing the door panels.

"What are you doing?" I demanded.

I got no answer. I was handed a clipboard with a paper to sign, and my keys.

"Excuse me, but why did you have the door panels removed?" I insisted.

"Our instructions. Just sign the paper, lady."

"I'm sure my attorney will be very interested in just exactly what your instructions were," I grumbled as I signed the form, scowled at him, and handed it back. Why would they take off the door panels? I decided not to dwell on it. I just wanted to *get out of Dodge*, before anything else happened.

It was two in the morning by the time I pulled into the marina parking lot. I let myself into the *Plan C* and turned on the lights. The message light on my answering machine flashed. I pressed the playback button and listened while I carried my overnight bag to my cabin.

The first four messages were from Craig: "Hi, sweetheart, it's me. Guess you're out. I'll try back later. . . . I love you." Beep. "Hi, Sweety. Me, again. Guess you're still out. . . . I miss you. . . . Nothing important. I'll call back. Love you." Beep. "Hello? Dev? Are you there? Guess not. . . . Where are you? I'll keep trying. I love you. 'Bye." Beep. "Devonie? What's going on? I've been trying to call you for two days. Where are you? I need to hear your voice. Uh. . . . I miss you. Are you there? Guess not. I'll keep trying. I love you. . . . Really."

I walked back to the phone and stared at the blinking lights. I couldn't deal with Craig at the moment. His questions demanded my undivided attention, and I had way too much going on at the moment to make decisions when it came to matters of the heart. I waited for the next message to play back.

"Devonie, it's Spencer. What're you into, girl? Call me as soon as you get in. I mean ASAP. Got it?"

I stared at the phone, then the clock. His voice had a definite urgency. I picked up the phone and dialed Spencer's number.

"Devonie! What the heck's going on? What are you mixed up in now?" Spencer barked into the phone.

"You know as much as I do. What happened?" I shot back.

"Some NSA guys were here today. They were submitting all kinds of queries. Came up with a rap sheet on you a mile long. It's a bunch of bogus stuff and I can prove it, but it really looks bad. You're in big trouble, Dev."

"What? NSA? Who's the NSA?"

"If you ask them, they'll tell you it stands for 'No Such Agency,' but don't believe it. It's the National Security Agency. These guys listen to the world's conversations and look for possible threats. They're probably listening to us right now. They're on you like stink on a skunk. You'd better get the heck out of there."

"Thanks, Spence. I'll catch up to you as soon as I can."

I dumped the contents of my overnight bag on my bed and threw some fresh clothes in it. I locked the *Plan C,* dashed up the dock to the parking area, and jumped into the Jeep. I peeled out of the parking lot.

The ATM machine was in a well-lit area, but I still felt uneasy. I checked over my shoulder before I slid my card into the slot. I punched in my PIN code and waited. I gaped at the "ACCOUNT CLOSED" message flashing on the small black screen. The machine kept my card. The thought of how they manipulated my bank records flashed through my mind. I didn't have time to ponder; I just knew I had to get the heck out of there.

I slowed down and coasted past the marina parking lot, without pulling in. The flashing red and yellow lights from five police cars parked at the marina office glared on the glass windows of my Jeep as it rolled by. I didn't stop.

Chapter Nine

I pulled to the curb in front of Jason's house and cut my lights and engine. A barking dog threatened to wake the neighborhood. I rifled through my tool kit for a screwdriver, then quietly opened my door.

Jason's vacationing neighbors just happened to own a Jeep Grand Cherokee, the same year as mine. The yuppie vehicle sat, unsuspectingly, in its dark driveway. I tiptoed to the back of the vehicle. My movements triggered a motion-detector light that flooded the driveway with a beam so bright I felt like a star on Broadway. I heard the sound of toenails clicking on the concrete walkway in the backyard. The black nose of Barney, the boxer, sniffed like a vacuum under the gate, and I could hear a low growl from deep in his throat. I crouched behind the Jeep, held my breath, and froze like a statute.

"It's okay, Barney. It's just me. I played tug-of-war with you while Jason fixed your dinner. Remember me?" I whispered.

Barney wasn't buying it. He let out a loud bark, then another. I quickly unscrewed the bolts holding the license plate to the bumper. Barney snarled between his frantic yelps. I jumped with every bark. I scooted around to the front of the Jeep and started on the second plate.

Jason's porch light flicked on. His front door opened, and I could see him step outside, wearing his robe and slippers. "Shush, Barney!" he ordered in the loudest whisper he could manage. Barney ignored his command.

"Darn you, Barney. You'll wake up the whole neighborhood," Jason complained.

I'd just removed the last screw from the license plate frame, when it slipped from my hands and fell to the ground. The noise startled Jason.

"Oh, jeez! Who's there?" he demanded, in a voice two octaves higher than normal.

I stood up, slowly. "It's just me, Jason. Don't call out the National Guard."

"Devonie? That you? What the heck are you doing?"

I gathered up the license plates and approached him. Barney continued to warn the world about the horrible thing happening in his owner's driveway.

I grabbed Jason's arm and ushered him toward his front door. "Let's go inside, so he'll be quiet."

"What are you doing?" he demanded.

"Don't be difficult; just come on, before he wakes up the whole block."

A half-dozen more barks after we'd closed the door, then Barney halted the neighborhood alert. I followed Jason into the kitchen and sat down at the table, laying the license plates in front of me.

"Alright. Tell me what's going on, or I'm giving Todd Schlempenheimer your phone number."

"No, not that. Anything but that." I grinned.

"Talk, girl."

"I've got to get to Sacramento. I've stirred up a hornet's nest with this stuff I got from Clancy. Somehow, someone's given me an electronic criminal history a mile long, and the state troopers are after me."

"What do you want with those plates?"

"I just want to put them on my Jeep, so I can get from here to Spencer's without being stopped."

"Jeez, Dev. I can't believe you're mixed up with something like this *again*."

"I know. Me either. Can I borrow some cash? They took my ATM card. I tried to use my gas card to fill up the Jeep, but my account's been closed. None of my credit cards are valid anymore. They're very thorough."

"Cash? How much?"

"As much as you can spare. I've got to get to Sacramento."

Jason disappeared into his bedroom, then returned with a glass mason jar. "Don't have much cash. You can have my poker money. There's probably about forty-five, maybe fifty bucks here."

My eyes bulged at the stash of coins. "All quarters?"

"It's cash. Want it or not?"

"Yes, I want it. It'll get me there. I'll eat light."

"I'll fix you something for the road. You won't have to worry about stopping for food."

"I can't bear the thought of one of your travel snacks. I'd rather go hungry."

"You'll change your tune about the time you get to Fresno. Your mouth'll water for one of my dill-pickle-and-peanut-butter sandwiches."

I cringed at the thought. "Don't you have apples or bananas? Any fruit at all?" I pleaded.

Jason tapped his chin with his finger, as he took a mental inventory of his cupboards. "Fruit? I've got some jam. I've got some grape bubblegum. Oh! I know! I've got a box of Frosted Strawberry Pop Tarts."

Jason slid open a drawer and pulled out a package. "Here. I was saving this for breakfast. You can have it. It's a Hostess Fruit Pie—berry. And I've got a six-pack of Orange Crush."

"This is your idea of fruit? You do realize real oranges don't come in aluminum cans with pop-tops, don't you?"

"I know. They come in paper cans you stick in the freezer until you mix 'em with water."

"Right," I smirked, then gathered up the license plates and Jason's care package and headed for the door.

I drove as far as I could, before my eyelids refused to stay open. I pulled into a rest area, crawled into the back of the Jeep, and immediately fell asleep. I woke up to the sound of my stomach growling. I put the Jeep in gear and headed down the road. I stopped to fill the tank, counting out twenty dollars in quarters to the cashier. I splurged and bought a bottle of water. By the time I passed the Fresno City Limit sign, the thought of Jason's pickle-and-peanut-butter sandwich actually sounded appetizing. He was right. Darn him, anyway. I stopped at a roadside fruit stand and bought a few apples to carry me through the rest of the trip.

Spencer wasn't home when I arrived. I didn't dare call him at work in case he was right about our phone conversations being listened to. I waited. Seven o'clock. No Spencer. Eight o'clock. Still no Spencer. Finally, at nine-thirty, the lights of his beat-up, old Dodge Dart reflected in my rear-view mirror, as he pulled into his driveway.

"Devonie! You made it. Quick, pull your Jeep into the garage. I'll meet you inside."

We sat down in front of Spencer's home computer system and powered the machine up.

"I exported the results of the criminal database query and e-mailed it to myself here. Look at this."

Spencer opened the file and displayed the results on the large seventeen-inch monitor. Each record contained personal information about me and a description of the crime I "allegedly" committed. "Whoever put these records in the database didn't count on anyone looking at the system-maintained fields. Every record is stamped with the system date and time. When I wrote this application, I made it impossible for anyone to modify the date stamp. I also store the IP address of the client machine making the entry," he explained.

My finger scanned down the "Date Added" column. Every date was the same—yesterday—and all the IP addresses were the same. "This was all entered yesterday by the same person," I noted.

Spencer pulled my finger off the screen and wiped the smudge off with a cloth. "Well, at least from the same machine. A real setup from the word, 'go.'"

"Can we find out who this IP address is assigned to?" I asked.

"Already working on it." Spencer made a few mouse clicks. "Look what I've been working on for the past six months: this is a graphical representation of the network I administer for the state. Every server, client, router, hub . . . you name it, I've got it documented here."

The screen looked like a street map of downtown San Francisco, only busier. I squinted my eyes to read the tiny print.

"Here, I'll zoom in." He clicked on the magnifying-glass icon and the area of interest became larger. "This IP address is assigned to a client machine at the U.S. Justice Department in Los Angeles—the building on South Soto Street, to be exact."

"Can you narrow it down to an office?" As usual, I was awed by Spencer's total mastery of the electronic world. There's no computer task he can't accomplish, given enough time and resources.

"Not with this tool. But I activated a protocol analyzer and set a capture filter on the IP address. Then, I spammed the L.A. office with an offer of cash for true stories with screenplay potential. Signed it *Spielberg*. All I had to do was sit back and wait for activity to pick up, and *voilà*! Got us a name to go with the IP address."

"Well? What is it?" I couldn't wait to hear.

"Carissa West." He beamed.

I ran the name through my own memory bank. "Carissa West? Doesn't sound familiar."

"Think we ought to send Carissa a message? Let her know we're on to her?" Spencer asked.

"Not yet. I think we should feed Carissa enough rope to hang herself with. As long as we make sure those database records aren't tampered with, you'll be able to come to my rescue with the evidence if I need it. Right?"

"Not to worry. I've made a backup of the export, and I've locked the record, so they can't be modified or deleted from the database."

"Good. By the way, can you do anything about getting my bank account reinstated? I'm gonna run out of quarters pretty soon."

"Probably could, but if I got caught, it'd back to the slammer."

"You're right. Forget I even suggested it." I hesitated a moment. "You have any spare cash?"

Chapter Ten

The bed in Spencer's guest room was comfortable enough, but I didn't sleep well. I tossed and turned all night, trying to piece together the puzzle I'd managed to unbox. Where was Gerald Bates? And why was his yacht sitting at the bottom of the ocean? Where was Roy Hastings? And why did he abandon his boat? Who was on my boat? And what were they looking for? Who was Carissa West? And why was she trying to frame me? Too many questions. No answers.

I couldn't lie there any longer. At six, I rolled out of bed and staggered down the hall to Spencer's living room. I searched for the remote and switched on the TV. There was no escaping the big news story of the week: the discovery of Gerald Bates's yacht. A news reporter stood on the deck of a commercial charter boat. In the background, two other boats were anchored. I could see divers leaping into the water.

The reporter brushed the wind-whipped hair from her face and pointed in the direction of the divers. "That's the exact spot where the *Gigabyte* went down. Getting to the wreck has been a major challenge for these divers, since the boat is down nearly one hundred and fifty feet. Reports so far indicate the yacht suffered major structural damage, most probably from a severe storm. Gerald Bates and his crew are presumed dead."

Spencer padded down the hallway in his Spiderman pajamas, scratching his head. "What'd they say caused it to sink?"

"They said it broke apart in a storm. Sure didn't look damaged when I saw it."

"Who said it broke apart?" Spencer asked.

"Don't know where that came from. They've got some divers going down to check it out." I squinted to get a better look at the boats in the background. "I can't tell for sure, but those don't look like Coast Guard boats."

Spencer studied the screen. "Could be divers hired by the Bates Corporation. Technically, that's who owns the yacht."

"Could be. You know, I bet Clancy knows exactly what's going on there. He was chomping at the bit to get the salvage contract. Maybe I'll give him a call." I found his number in my purse and dialed Spencer's phone. No answer. I checked my watch. "No wonder. It's not even seven yet. I'll try later. What's for breakfast?"

Spencer marched into the kitchen and opened a cabinet. I listened as he proudly called out my choices. "I've got Cheerios, Frosted Flakes, Lucky Charms, Fruit Loops, and, my favorite, Captain Crunch."

I mulled over the choices. "Got anything that doesn't list sugar as the first ingredient?"

There was a long silence. "Want me to cook you something?" Spencer offered.

"Cook? You cook?" I asked.

"Toast sound good?"

"Wheat?"

"Wonder. White."

"Fruit?"

"Raisins. Old."

"How about going out to eat. I'll buy."

"How are you going to do that? You don't have any money or credit cards."

"Right. How about we go out, and you buy?"

"Okay. McDonald's?"

"Try again."

"Burger King? McDonalds?" He struggled.

"Okay. How's this for a plan: We go to the grocery store; I pick out the food; you pay; we bring it back here and I fix breakfast."

"None of that tofu junk. Promise?"

"Promise. No tofu."

"Okay."

After breakfast, I tried Clancy's number again. Still no answer. I checked my watch. "That's weird. He should be in by now."

I called information and got his home number. No answer there, either.

"Maybe they're on vacation. People have been known to do that, you know," Spencer offered.

"Maybe. I'm going to check the news again."

I turned on the set and watched as the camera panned the media scene. The reporter stuck a microphone in the face of a tall, mustached man. I did a double take, as the familiar man answered her questions.

"That's him. That's Morgan Johnson," I blurted.

"Who's Morgan Johnson?"

"He's an insurance investigator. He was with me when we found the *Gigabyte*."

Our eyes were glued to the TV as Morgan answered the reporter's questions. "Yes. I've made a couple preliminary dives. There's a split in a section of the hull—likely a defect in the structural material. A massive storm, similar to *El Niño*, probably stressed it beyond its capacity," Morgan explained.

"I don't remember seeing anything like that. But, he *is* the expert. Does this for a living. I'm sure he knows what he's talking about," I tried to convince myself.

"What insurance agency does he work for?" Spencer asked.

"West Coast Insurance. They must be the carrier for the *Gigabyte*. That'll be some huge claim. Bet they'll be crying the blues."

Spencer chuckled. "You kidding? That's a drop in the bucket for them. Hey, while you were doing the dishes, I logged into the DOJ network and ran a check on Carissa West. Her father is Harlan West—big shot with the NSA. Whatever's going on, I bet those two are in it up to their eyeballs. I still think we ought to rattle her cage a little."

"Not yet. We don't know enough about her," I warned.

"I called the office. Told them I'd be working from home today. Let's go see what else we can dig up on Carissa."

I pulled up a chair next to Spencer as he sat in front of his computer and cracked his fingers like a pianist preparing to play Mozart.

"Always said you can find out a lot about a person

by reading their mail. Let's see what kind of e-mail little Miss Carissa gets," Spencer said.

I watched the clock in the bottom corner of the screen. In less than five minutes, Spencer had hacked into the e-mail server for the U.S. Justice Department and was scrolling down a list of user ID's.

"There she is: 'Cwest.' Now, let's find her mailbox," Spencer announced proudly. A few more keystrokes and he was in. "Bingo. Where should we start?"

My eyes scrolled down the list of documents. "Let's sort it by sender."

"Done. Look. There's something from dear old dad."

"Good. Let's open it," I directed.

The correspondence began with Harlan's request to Carissa:

Tuesday-8:00am-sender:hwest—Carissa: I need your help on something. Devonie Lace, from San Diego, is on the road right now. I need her picked up ASAP and her vehicle searched by our team. Be creative. I don't know where she is, except that she's not at home.

Tuesday-8:10am-sender:cwest—Okay. Do we hold her indefinitely?

Tuesday-8:12am-sender:hwest—No. Just search the vehicle. We're looking for film or pictures or a camera.

Tuesday-7:00pm-sender:cwest—picked her up. Searched the vehicle. Nothing. What now?

Tuesday-8:00pm-sender:hwest—Okay. Let's pick her up again. This time make it stick. We've got to find out what she has. Don't give her a way out.

Wednesday-5:00pm-sender:cwest—She's on the run. We haven't located her yet. Instructions?

Wednesday-7:00pm-sender:hwest—Meet me in San Francisco at the Bates Building tomorrow at 3:00pm. I'll need your help to check out Bates's computer. We need to make sure no files can link him to us.

"Wednesday," I blurted. "That was yesterday. They'll be in San Francisco today at three. Can we get in there, first?" I asked.

Spencer hit a few control keys and cleared the screen. "Hack into the Bates Corporation system? I've heard they got a team of top network people there dedicated to the complete eradication of the hacker species as we know it."

"You don't think you can do it?" I challenged.

"Oh, I can do it, but it'll take some time. Just don't know if I can get it done before three."

"Well, let's give it a try. I have confidence in you."

Spencer frantically typed commands on his keyboard and waited for responses to display on the screen. "Jeez! These guys are good! Some firewall they've built. Let me try running this password database by it."

I watched the clock. Twenty minutes passed and we hadn't even gotten through the firewall. It was past ten and it would take three hours to drive to San Francisco.

"Okay. Plan B. Can you get us into the Bates I.T. department? Maybe use your connection with the State?" I asked.

"Maybe. Careful as they are, it'd surprise me if we get anything. Sure like to meet the man in charge down there. Really knows his stuff."

"Good. I'll be ready in five minutes. Let's take my Jeep. Just want to try Clancy one more time."

I picked up the phone and dialed. Still no answer.

Chapter Eleven

The Bates Corporation building was one of those glass towers that looks like it belongs in the Emerald City. Bates Corporation stock prices had climbed steadily since it went public back in the early '80s. Even with Gerald Bates, "the wizard behind the curtain," missing, the momentum of the machine just kept on going. I followed Spencer through the glass entrance into the reception area.

"Good afternoon. I'm Spencer Davis, State of California. This is my assistant." Spencer motioned toward me. "I have an appointment with Dave, your Network Administrator."

The receptionist smiled at us, then referred to a chart taped to the panel under the raised counter. "Dave? Do you have a last name?"

Spencer turned to me. "You made the appointment. What's the last name?"

I didn't hide the helplessness in my face. I shrugged my shoulders. "I don't remember. I don't think he told me his last name."

Spencer's voice became surprisingly firm. "You don't remember? Or he didn't tell you? Which is it?"

"Uh . . . I don't remember?" I squeaked pathetically.

"Are you even sure his name was Dave?" Spencer pressed.

"Well . . . I think . . . I'm not totally—"

"That's it! What've you got—Jell-O for brains? You've embarrassed me for the last—"

"Wait," the receptionist interrupted. "You must mean Stan Parker. He's our network administrator. I don't see you on his calendar, but I can buzz him. You're from the State?"

I breathed a sigh of relief. The receptionist shot me a sympathetic glance that told me she was all too familiar with ogres like Spencer. *Jell-O for brains?* That wasn't part of the script. I'd have to have a talk with Spencer on the way home.

"That's right. Spencer Davis."

She whispered a few words into her headset, then gave us a big smile. "He'll be right up. Go ahead and have a seat."

Stan Parker led us past dozens of cubicles, down endless corridors, along windowed offices, and finally, to a room he called his office. We each took a seat opposite his desk and smiled pleasantly.

"What can I do for you, Mr. Davis?" Stan began.

"Call me Spencer. I'm doing some benchmarking of our network security. I've been informed your security measures have made your network nearly bulletproof. I was hoping you'd show us around—let us take a look at what you've done."

"I see. Unfortunately, I somehow failed to scheduled our appointment on my calendar. I have an appointment at three I can't get out of, but maybe I can just field some questions? That be okay?"

"I guess that would work. Could you give us a brief tour of your equipment room? Nothing fancy, just a look-see?" Spencer negotiated.

"I think I can arrange that," Stan offered.

"Great. Well, why don't you start by explaining how you set up the architecture for your firewall."

"Firewall?" Stan asked.

"Yes. I understand it's nearly un-hackable. How did you go about setting it up?" Spencer asked, with a confident tone to his voice.

Stan tapped a pencil on his desk. His eyes darted around the few papers he had neatly placed in the corner of his workstation. "You know, I've got a flow chart of that around here somewhere. Why don't I see if I can dig it up and send you a copy. Can you give me your business card?"

"Sure. Here you go." Spencer handed him his official State-of-California card. "Flow chart? That'd be great. How about your modem server? You have a flow chart for that, too?"

"Sure, we do. We have flow charts for everything," Stan boasted. "I'll make copies of all of them for you."

"Well, this is wonderful. How about pseudo code? Have any of that you can part with? Just the code related to your network security would be sufficient. And if you have any Cobol source code, that'd be perfect," Spencer requested.

"Pseudo code? Cobol source code? Of course. I'll include that in the package. Let me just make a list for my assistant. Anything else?"

Spencer shot me a quick glance. I checked my watch. It was nearly two-thirty. "Can't think of anything else . . . except that tour you promised."

"Certainly. Follow me. It's upstairs."

We followed Stan into an elevator and waited for the doors to open on the second floor. We walked past another row of cubicles, then down a long hallway. "Right through here." He pushed open a large glass door.

Two hardware technicians were busy setting up a workstation. Empty computer boxes and Styrofoam packing materials were strewn around the room, waiting for the cleaning crew to haul them away.

Stan pointed to a rack with ten computer monitors stacked on two shelves. The ten servers were packed tightly on the bottom shelf of the rack. Spencer whistled, as only an impressed computer geek could. "Cool. Very cool."

Stan smiled. "We try to keep everything very neat and organized here."

"It shows. Can I walk around the back?" Spencer's eyes lit up like a kid in a candy store.

"Sure. Come on back."

Spencer took a step, then tripped over a stray piece of Styrofoam. He caught himself on his knees, then pushed his glasses back up on his nose. "Jeez! What a klutz I am. Let me just toss this, so no one else trips over it." Spencer picked up the spongy object. Still on his knees, he placed it in a garbage can sitting next to the rack. He stood up, brushed himself off, and proceeded to the back of the rack.

"What you got back here, Stan? Holy cow! Is that all fiber?"

Spencer went on for ten minutes, admiring the cabling and hardware. Finally, I peeked around the corner of the rack. "Mr. Davis? I think it's time to get back to the office. We have a long drive, and Mr. Parker has that other appointment."

Spencer looked at his watch. "Right you are. I completely lost track of the time. Thanks for letting me see this work of art, Stan."

"You bet. Glad I could be of help," Stan replied.

We followed Stan back to the reception area. I noticed a stack of *Bates Corporation Newsletters* on a table in the waiting room. I picked one up on our way out.

"Feel like driving?" I asked.

"Sure. Got the keys?"

I handed the keys to Spencer and walked around to the passenger-side door.

Spencer laughed so hard, he could barely buckle his seatbelt. "You pick up on it?"

I joined Spender in his laugh-fest. "The flow chart business? And the pseudo code! What was he talking about?"

"That guy is no more a network administrator than I'm the Queen of England. You like the Cobol touch I added? He wouldn't know the front end of a server if it kicked him in the back end. I'm surprised he could find the computer room."

"Doesn't matter. Looks like we struck out, anyway. We're no further ahead than we were this morning," I pointed out.

Spencer grinned and reached into his pocket. "Not necessarily. Look what I found digging through the trash." He pulled a mini data cartridge tape from his pocket and handed it to me. It was labeled, "BAD TAPE."

"What's this?" I asked, inspecting the tape.

"It's a backup tape. They go bad after a while and usually just get tossed. Check out the last backup date."

I read down the short list. The most recent date was only two weeks old. "But it's bad. How can we use it?"

Spencer gave me his usual "leave it to me" grin.

"You can read this?" I asked.

"Can a duck swim?"

"Hmm . . . good. Maybe we're not up a creek after all."

"Oh, we're up a creek, alright—but at least we have a paddle."

I handed the tape back to Spencer and began leafing through the pages of the *Bates Corporation Newsletter*.

The first page was dedicated to the corporate mission statement. It all sounded good. Mission statements always sound good. As I read it aloud, Spencer quietly hummed the "Star Spangled Banner" in the background.

I flipped through more pages. Employee birthdays and anniversaries were listed on several pages. Photos from a recent employee retirement banquet took up a couple more. Four pages were dedicated to show off the new layout for the company's commonly-used forms—now designed to be more user-friendly and efficient.

I turned, once more, to a full double-page layout, featuring a photo of Gerald Bates shaking hands with an Arab businessman. The caption, printed in big, bold letters, stood out against the black-and-white photo:

"Bates Goes East: Out With the Old (Oil), In With the New (Technology)."

"Listen to this . . ." I read excerpts of the article to Spencer. "Gerald Bates travels to Baghdad to participate in a series of meetings with Iraqi oil industrialist, Mohammed Aziz. The focus of the meetings are to discuss the future of computer technology in a country Bates has been known to openly criticize for its 'mono-industry' mentality."

Spencer chuckled. "They may be 'mono-industrial,' but boy, what an industry. Two million barrels of oil a day can feed a lot of camels. Wasn't there some kind of sanction on Iraq after the Gulf War? They could only trade oil for food or something?"

"Yeah. Listen to this: it says Bates contacted Aziz, after he'd announced he'd lost millions in revenues due to the sanctions. Bates suggested a partnership, of sorts, where the Iraqi company would diversify its efforts and begin assembling certain computer components."

"Did Aziz go for it?" Spencer asked.

"I don't know. According to this, more meetings were scheduled until Bates disappeared. The talks stopped after that. Wasn't it just a few days after Bates returned from some Middle-Eastern country that he vanished?" I asked.

"One day; he'd only been back for a day. He landed in San Francisco on a Sunday and never showed up for work on Monday morning. No one's seen him since," Spencer replied.

I turned the page and continued reading the story. "Huh? This is weird."

"What?" Spencer asked.

"It couldn't be, could it?" I continued.

"What?" Spencer demanded. "What?"

"Here are some pictures from one of his trips to Baghdad. Stan Parker is with him in a couple."

"Our Stan Parker? Mr. Flow Chart?"

"One and the same. Only he's not listed as a network administrator. The caption here says he's an aide to Mr. Bates. Would a change from CEO Aide to Network Administrator be considered a promotion or a demotion, I wonder?"

"Depends on if he got a pay cut or a pay raise, I guess," Spencer contemplated.

"This whole thing is too weird. What do you think we'll find when we get to the bottom of it?"

"*If* we get to the bottom of it."

"If? Come on, Spence. If we don't solve this, I can't ever go home, and I'll have to mooch off you forever. We *have* to solve it."

"Right. *When* we get to the bottom of it."

Chapter Twelve

I counted the rings of the telephone: twelve. Clancy still didn't pick up—and neither did an answering machine. I began to worry about him. He'd been so anxious to pursue the salvage contract on the *Gigabyte;* maybe he'd been too persistent. I hung up the phone and stared out the window.

Spencer walked through the door and dropped a wad of crisp twenty-dollar bills on the coffee table. "Here. Two hundred bucks. That get you by?"

"Thanks, Spence. You're a lifesaver."

"Get through to your friend yet?"

"No, I'm really worried. Think I oughta get back to San Diego to see if I can find him. Maybe there's just a problem with his phone."

"Think it's safe to go back? You know they're looking for you," he warned.

"I know. I won't go back to the boat. I'll find someplace to hole up. There're more than a million people living in San Diego. Shouldn't be too hard to get lost in the crowd."

"Be careful just the same. I'll get everything I can off this backup tape. How will I get in touch with you?"

"I'll call you," I promised.

Three rows of worry lines creased Spencer's forehead. I'd never seen him this concerned, even when he was being investigated for criminal computer-record tampering. I gave him a big smile and draped my arm over his shoulders.

"Don't you worry about me. I've been through worse than this," I assured him.

"It's not that. I just want to make sure I get my two hundred dollars back." He grinned as he squeezed my hand.

I punched him in the arm.

"Ouch!"

"Ouch?" I barely touched you, you wimp."

"I'm no wimp. Just sensitive, that's all."

"Sorry. Hey, thanks for all your help. I'd really be in deep you-know-what without a shovel if it weren't for you."

"No problem. Just get out of here and let me get busy on this tape, okay?"

"Okay."

I parked the Jeep in a public lot near Clancy's place. It looked a little out of place between the bondo-gray Volkswagen bus and the empty boat trailer with two flat tires, but for free parking, it would do.

I expected to see Tex, the happy-go-lucky golden retriever, gallop up the dock to greet me, but he didn't. The only sign that Tex ever existed was the fuzzy yellow tennis ball sitting in an otherwise empty bucket next to the front entrance. The door to the salvage office was locked up tight—no sign of life anywhere. I peered through the dirty window. It was dark inside. Olive's computer monitor sat lifeless on her desk, framed by a dozen little yellow sticky notes. Tex's dog blanket was piled next to the desk.

I walked around and checked all the windows. Everything was sealed up tight; no way to get in without breaking something. I peered down the dock. Clancy's boat was gone, but the *Little Maria* was still tied up.

I walked down the dock. There was no one around to stop me from climbing onboard. The key chain dangled from the ignition. I checked the fuel level, started the engine, and untied the lines.

I'd watched Clancy operate the GPS, and with a few presses of the buttons, I'd managed to get on course for the *Gigabyte* wreck site.

The seas were a little choppy; I was glad I hadn't eaten. I wanted to make the cash Spencer gave me last as long as possible; otherwise, I'd be forced to turn to Jason's culinary adventures.

As I neared the wreck site, I saw the outline of a boat on the horizon. I searched all the drawers and cabinets for binoculars, but couldn't find any. As I got closer, I slowed down and squinted to get a better look. I could see some activity on the boat—people moving about. It looked like two, maybe three; I couldn't be sure. I advanced closer—close enough, I decided.

The outline of a rifle was unmistakable. A man perched at the stern rested the gun on his shoulder as he kept watch of the area. These people were serious. The presence of armed guards confirmed my suspicions that there may be more than a big fancy yacht sitting down there. No unauthorized persons would be venturing down to get a closer look at the *Gigabyte*.

One thing was sure: if I could see them with the naked eye, they could certainly see me. And they'd be watching me closely to see what I was up to. I dropped the anchor and went below. There I found a fishing pole, carried it up to the deck, and cast out the line. I secured it to the railing and glanced over at the other boat. They had to be watching me. Hopefully, I looked innocent enough.

I went below again and grabbed a full scuba tank, then returned to the deck. I'd positioned the boat so that I could gear up on the opposite side of the fly-bridge where they couldn't see me. I inserted the mouthpiece, eased myself into the water, and began my descent to about twenty feet. I continued in the direction of the other boat, surfaced directly under the bow, and listened.

"You sure she's still fishing?" I heard one of the guards ask.

"Yeah. The line's still out. Don't get your shorts in a knot," the other replied.

I slipped back under the surface and found their anchor line. I hoped they'd dropped anchor close to the wreck site, but there was no way to be sure. I followed the line down to the bottom. The powerful beam from my flashlight was lost in the murky water. I made gradually larger circles around the anchor as I searched for the boat. Keenly aware of my time limit, I checked my watch every couple of minutes.

The bright white light bounced back at me as it found its mark. I advanced on the wreck and quickly made my way around its perimeter. I shone the light on the entire surface, looking for the structural damage that, supposedly, sent it to the bottom. After two passes around it, I was convinced there was no damage. Not a hole, not a break, not even a hairline crack was evident.

Too soon, my time was up. I found the anchor line and slowly made my way back to the surface.

The crew on the guard boat had grown suspicious.

"When was the last time you actually saw her on deck?" one of them demanded.

"I don't know. Maybe ten or fifteen minutes ago," the other answered. "I think you're worried about nothing." His voice sounded as if he were eating.

"I want to check it out. Pull up the anchor."

"Can I finish my sandwich first?" the other whined.

I slipped under the surface and raced for the *Little Maria*. It felt like the dream I have where I'm trying to run away from danger but can only move in slow motion. My heart raced as I frantically kicked my flippers through the water. Though only minutes passed, it seemed like it took hours to reach the *Little Maria*. I struggled to hoist myself up the ladder and over the rail, but all the scuba gear was just too heavy for me. My hands were shaking and I didn't have the strength to pull myself up. All I could do was drop the tank and weight belt and let them sink to the bottom. I threw the flippers over the rail and climbed up the ladder. I could hear the engine of the approaching boat as I crawled on my belly to the cabin and slithered inside. I unzipped the wet suit and frantically struggled to get out of it, then rolled it up and pushed it in the corner.

"Anyone onboard?" I heard someone call as their boat pulled next to mine. I shook the water out of my hair and walked out on deck.

"I'm here," I announced. "What can I do for you?"

The two men were young, probably in their mid-twenties. The man at the wheel was tall and muscular. He wore a blue-and-white striped T-shirt with an embroidered anchor on the breast pocket. His long, stringy blond hair was windblown and hung in his eyes. It reminded me of an Old English sheepdog; I wished he would comb it back, so I could see his eyes. The other man, a head shorter than his partner and about twenty pounds heavier, wore a bright-yellow windbreaker. He was busy stuffing his mouth with marshmallows that he pulled from a bag sitting on one of the passenger seats. To my relief, I didn't see any rifles.

"You been swimming out here?" the taller one asked.

"Yeah. I just took a quick dip to cool off. The water's great," I answered.

"You alone?" he continued interrogating.

"Yeah. Why?"

The marshmallow-eater jammed the last of the puffy, white blobs into his already-full mouth, reminding me of a chipmunk. I tried not to focus on the little bits of sugary, white paste that flew out of his mouth as he spoke. "How's the fishing? Catch anything?"

I glanced over at the pole propped against the railing. It was motionless. "No. Nothing biting today."

"What're you using?" he asked after finally swallowing the mass of confection stuffed in his mouth.

"Using?" I echoed.

"Bait. What are you using for bait?" he asked as he

wadded up his empty marshmallow bag and tossed it over the side into the water.

I wanted to jump across the rail and wrap my fingers around his big, thoughtless, ocean-polluting throat, but I remembered the rifle, and kept my politically correct speech to myself. I turned my head and ignored the marshmallow bag floating next to my boat.

"I picked up a bucket of sardines this morning. Gotta use 'em before they go belly-up on me."

"Live bait? What're you after?" the taller one chimed in.

"Bass ... maybe tuna or yellowtail. Don't know if albacore are running yet, but I wouldn't mind snagging one of those. I heard marshmallow makes good bait but looks like you guys are all out," I commented, nodding toward the floating plastic bag that had, by now, drifted twenty feet from my stern.

They looked at each other and shrugged their shoulders.

"You sure you're out here alone?" the taller one asked, ignoring my observation of his partner's litter.

"Just me and my boat. What're you guys doing out here?"

"You been watching the news?" marshmallow man asked.

"News? No. Too depressing. Did something happen? Did I miss a war?" I laughed a nervous laugh.

They both returned phony chuckles. The taller one matched my lie with one of his own. "Nah. We're just fishing, too. Wondered if you caught anything. You better be careful swimming out here, especially if you're gonna have live bait on the end of your line." His plastic smile turned to a serious frown. "Sharks won't think twice about stealing your catch, and if you're splashing around out there, who knows what else they'll take."

I studied his face to determine if it was a friendly warning or a threat he had just given me. "Thanks. I'll keep that in mind," I called back, with all the sincerity of an iguana.

They started their engine and retreated to their original position. I waved a couple times and they waved back.

I reeled in my unbaited line and snagged the empty marshmallow bag with the tip of my pole, so I could dispose of it properly.

I shaded my eyes and peered up at the sun, almost directly overhead. It would take over two hours to get back to Long Beach, but I estimated I could be in Catalina in just a little over an hour. Roy Hastings hailed from Avalon, on the east side of the island. I figured it couldn't hurt to snoop around a little and besides, I was starving.

Chapter Thirteen

As I approached the marina at Avalon, I could see there were no docks to tie up to. A fellow sailor directed me to a buoy and offered me dinghy service to the dock. Studying the boats berthed in the marina, the diversity of class was painfully evident. A beautiful eighty-foot yacht was tethered directly next to a tiny, paint-peeling, wood-rotting, barely-afloat scow.

I turned around on the bench seat in the dinghy and addressed my chauffeur. "You know Roy Hastings?" I asked.

"Roy who?"

"Hastings. He used to live around here."

"I'm new to the island. Don't know too many folks yet. You say his name's Roy Hastings?"

"Yes. He ran a charter service. Just wondered if you knew him."

"Sorry. Maybe some other folks'll know him." He cut the engine to his tiny boat, and we drifted to a small platform built out from the shore for tying up the dinghies.

"Well, here we are. Watch your step."

I thanked him and climbed out of the little craft onto the dock.

I felt the weight of a man staring from the pier. His

gaze made me uneasy, but there was no escaping it. He paralleled me on the pier as I rushed up the dock. The quicker I walked, the more he picked up his pace. He was an older man, maybe in his early sixties. He wore a pair of khaki shorts and a Hawaiian shirt. His hair was mostly gray, and worn in a ponytail. He was tall and slender and in good condition—maybe a swimmer, from the looks of him. He intersected my path and stood squarely in front of me.

"What're you doin' with that boat?" he demanded.

I didn't know what to say. I shrugged my shoulders. "Boat?"

"Yeah! What are you doin' with Roy's boat?" he repeated.

"Oh, Roy's boat. You know him?"

"Just answer the question. Roy's been missing for six months, and now you show up with his boat. Where'd you get it?" he persisted.

"Well, a marine salvager over in Long Beach found it abandoned, and claimed it. I borrowed it for the day. Thinking of buying it."

"Buying it? Roy's boat?" he questioned.

"That's right. You know Roy?"

"I do . . . I did. Like I say, haven't seen him for six months. What's the name of the salvage outfit?"

"Tex and Clancy's. My name's Devonie Lace. And you are . . . ?"

"Huh? Oh, Sherman. Name's Sherman."

"Good to meet you, Sherman. You know Roy well?"

"One of my best friends. Really miss the old crab. Where'd they find his boat?"

"Don't know for sure. Somewhere south of here,

just adrift. Clancy figures he was diving alone—maybe ran into sharks."

Sherman digested what I'd said. He stared out at the *Little Maria,* tied to her buoy. "He wasn't alone," he stated.

When relying on pure chance, I estimate that ninety-nine percent of the time, I don't get what I hope for. When I started out for Catalina, I had hoped to find some answers about Roy Hastings, but I really only expected to get lunch. I stared at Sherman and realized this may be one of those one-percent moments. I shook the flood of a thousand questions out of my head and moved a little closer to make sure I heard him correctly. "What?"

"I said, he wasn't alone," he barked at me.

I glanced up the sidewalk to a row of waterside restaurants. "Sherman, you had lunch yet?"

The sun warmed my shoulders as we sat at a small table overlooking the marina. I peered over the railing and watched a garibaldi fish swim in the shallow water under the deck of the restaurant. At first sight, I thought it was the only fish down there. Then I strained to focus, I discovered dozens of fish swimming around; they were just more camouflaged than the bright-orange one that caught my attention. I was reminded of how easy it is to disappear into the scenery when you're not different enough to draw attention to yourself. I made a mental note to keep this observation fresh in my mind—I needed to blend into the background.

I offered to buy Sherman's lunch, hoping he'd go for something inexpensive since I was on a tight budget. Amy, our waitress, patiently waited, while Sherman studied the menu.

"Fish and chips, Amy," he ordered.

My eyes quickly scanned down the menu selections. "I'll have a small salad."

Amy took our menus and walked away.

"Tell me what you know about the day Roy disappeared," I began.

"I know he wasn't alone. Remember it like it was yesterday. Had a heck of a storm that night. Crazy Roy set out to open sea to keep his boat from gettin' beat against the rocks. Came back all excited about some wreck he'd found. Went on and on about it. I run a dive shop in town. Handled a lot of Roy's charters. Sure do miss him."

Sherman gulped down the glass of water Amy brought. He set it back down, then played with an ice cube at the bottom of the glass with his spoon. I watched him for a full minute and wondered what was so fascinating about the ice.

"What about this wreck?" I pressed.

"Oh, yeah. Said it was a real fancy yacht—rich fellow must've owned it. He knew it went down in the storm, 'cause he'd seen it during the night still afloat."

"How did he know it sank?" I asked.

"Found stuff floating—deck chairs and . . ." Sherman glanced up at the sky and tapped his finger on the side of his face. ". . . something . . . weird. What was it? Oh yeah, computer mouse pads. He used his sonar equipment to locate the wreck. Came in all excited about pictures he took. A customer in my shop was real interested and hired Roy to take him the next day to check it out. I filled his tanks and left 'em out back for him. That was the last I ever saw of Roy."

The sound of Paddy's carbon-monoxide-detector alarm flashed through my mind. Could Sherman have contaminated his friend's tanks by mistake? Or on purpose? "You filled his tanks?" I asked, studying his face carefully as he answered.

"Yeah. Filled 'em the night before, 'cause they were leavin' real early in the morning," Sherman explained.

He seemed sincere, but I've been known to be wrong about people. I decided to ask the question. "You ever have a problem with carbon monoxide contamination in the tanks you fill?"

Sherman shook his head. "Nope. Never. Too smart to do somethin' that dumb."

I nodded and took a sip from my water glass. "You don't happen to remember the man's name, do you?"

"Heck no. Didn't think much of it at the time. You know how it is. If I'd known I'd never see Roy again, I'd have paid more attention."

"How about what he looked like? Or if he was with someone? Anything stand out?" I pressed.

Sherman stared into the sky, searching his memory. "Don't recall too much of what he looked like. Just a regular fellow—no scars or tattoos to make him stand out. Don't think he was on the island alone 'cause I saw him at the marina with four or five other guys that morning. They'd just gotten off a boat. I was out checking the damage from the terrible storm that night."

"Four or five others? But only one went with Roy?"

"Only one I know of. Don't know what happened with the others. Didn't see them again."

"Where did Roy live?"

"Had a little place up on Whittley. Still empty. He owned it outright. No relatives. I figure the state'll take it for taxes eventually—if Roy don't show up."

"Would you show me where it is?"

"I suppose. Why you so interested?"

I wasn't prepared to give out any more information about what I knew. If I told Sherman that the tanks he'd filled were full of poison gas, he'd either clam up and go into denial, or he'd call in the cavalry. Neither option looked good to me at the moment. "Oh, I'm just curious to know what happened to him. Don't you think it's strange, him disappearing like that?"

Sherman nodded his head as he took a big bite out of his deep-fried fish. Tartar sauce dripped down his chin. He either didn't realize it was there, or he didn't care, because he left the white glob on his face. I fought an uncontrollable urge to wipe it off.

We stood on the front porch of the little clapboard house. Sherman noticed me staring at the white paint that was just beginning to peel.

"I was gonna help Roy paint her this summer, but . . ."

I nodded my head. He didn't need to explain. I pulled the ring of keys from my purse and searched for one that looked like it might fit the front door.

"Where'd you get those?" Sherman asked.

"They were on the *Little Marina.* Maybe one fits." I tried several, but with no luck.

"Try that one." Sherman pointed to an inconspicuous-looking key marked, "Black and Decker."

I slid it into the lock and turned the key. Bingo. We were in.

The house was dark and musty; smelled like the windows hadn't been opened for at least six months. I flipped a light switch, but nothing happened. I assumed the electricity had been turned off for some time, since Roy wasn't around to pay the bills. The drapes were closed. I opened them to let in some light.

There were dirty dishes in the sink and a line of ants crawled along the counter, feasting on the meal of the century. A few stacks of papers littered the kitchen table. I fingered through a few envelopes until a small slip of paper caught my eye. I picked it up and studied the blue letters on bright-yellow paper. It was a photo-processing claim-check, dated November tenth. I glanced around to make sure Sherman wasn't watching and slipped the paper in my pocket.

A half-dozen wet suits hung from a bar in the doorway between the living room and a bedroom. They each had some sort of rip or tear and required patching. Two scuba tanks sat in one corner, and a bunch of snorkels and masks were piled in the other.

Four fishing poles, of various heights and gauges, leaned against a wall next to a book shelf. I scanned the titles: not much fiction, except for copies of *The Old Man and The Sea* and *Moby Dick*. The others were either about boats, diving, or fishing, and a few on carpentry.

Sherman looked at his watch. "You know, I gotta get back to my shop. You seen all you want?"

"Think I could stay and look around?" I coaxed.

"Don't think it's a good idea. Neighbors might shoot you."

"That wouldn't be good. Can we come back later?" I asked.

"I'll see. Maybe after I close up shop."

We locked the house and climbed back into Sherman's golf cart—one of the main forms of transportation on the island—and headed back to town.

"What time do you close your shop?" I asked.

"About five. Come by after that if you're still interested."

The lady behind the counter at the drugstore gave me a big smile. She reminded me of my Aunt Margie—before the electrolysis. "Yeah. This is one of our claim checks. Older than Methuselah. You forget about it?" she questioned.

I have a difficult time with lying, even when I know it's necessary for my own self-preservation. I'm convinced my nose grows a little with each fib, so if I can answer in an almost-truthful way, I try. "Sort of," I replied.

"Well, let me see if we still have them." She fingered through a pile of envelopes haphazardly thrown in a drawer. "You're in luck," she said, pulling an envelope out. "Hey, these are Roy's pictures. You know Roy?"

"I'm his sister," I said, as I glanced all around the counter, but never directly at her. "He asked me to pick them up for him."

She ran her eyes up and down my body. "Roy never mentioned a sister. You from around here?"

I nonchalantly reached my hand to my nose and pretended to scratch it. No, it didn't feel any bigger than usual. "Long Beach," I answered. That, at least, was half true.

"Haven't seen Roy for—gosh, it's been months. He okay?" she asked.

"Fine. The pictures?" I reminded her.

"Oh. Sure. Here ya go, hon. That'll be fifteen, eighty-three."

I handed her $20 and waited while she counted out my change. I wandered back outside and found a bench overlooking the beach. I sat down and tore open the envelope.

Even in the dark, murky, underwater photos, I recognized the familiar image of the *Gigabyte*. I'd seen it firsthand, but hadn't gone inside the wreck. I stared at the photos of the main salon, the galley, and the cabins. What a beautiful yacht. I thought of my *Plan C* and hoped she was safe and sound in her slip; the explosion of my first boat, the *Plan B,* flashed uneasily through my mind. The sickening feeling I had when I saw her go up in flames edged its way to the front of my memory.

I thumbed through a couple of photos that reinforced the bad feeling I had about the demise of the *Gigabyte*. I wasn't exactly sure what I was looking at. Something about it looked familiar, but what? I studied the photos a while longer. It couldn't be what it looked like; the poor lighting must have played a trick on the camera. Or maybe not.

I jogged back-down to the marina and hitched a dinghy ride to the *Little Maria.*

The sun was just dipping below the horizon as I tied up to the dock in Long Beach. I dug my cell phone out of my purse and punched in Spencer's number. I hoped he'd found some answers to why all this was happening to me.

"Hey, Spencer. It's me. What'd you come up with?"

"Dev? You okay?" I sensed a level of concern in his voice.

"Fine. What did you find out?"

"You won't believe it . . . but I really don't think we should talk about it over the phone. Understand?" His voice took on a low, *James-Bondish* tone. I smiled at the thought of Spencer playing super-spy.

"Yeah. I get it. What do you want to do?"

"I'm gonna catch a flight out of here in the morning. Can you pick me up at LAX?" he asked.

"Yeah. What time?" I said, grabbing a pencil to write down the information.

"Ten-thirty. Southwest."

"Okay. See you then," I said, then powered off my phone.

I rolled my sleeping bag out on the floor in the lower hold of the *Little Maria*. I laid on my back, staring at the ceiling, and wondered where Clancy and Olive might be. I hoped Spencer was right, and they just decided to take a vacation. A little voice in my head told me that that probably wasn't the case.

I thought of calling my FBI friend, Dan Cooper. I knew I could trust him. Maybe after I talked to Spencer tomorrow, I'd call Dan.

My stomach growled as I tried to drift off to sleep; I'd forgotten to eat dinner.

Chapter Fourteen

I was only twenty miles from the Los Angeles International Airport, but when I got to the 405 freeway, I may as well have been half-a-world away. I merged into the quagmire of traffic and tried to make my way over to the far left lane.

"You people are crazy to do this every day," I announced to no one. I watched the seemingly infinite number of commuters curse as they cut each other off, and exchanged dirty looks and internationally-recognized gestures of total irritation. "It's no wonder you're all shooting at each other on the freeways." I read the bumper sticker on the pickup truck in front of me: "Cover me—I'm changing lanes."

It would have been easier to find a parking spot at the mall on the Saturday before Christmas than it was to find one at the airport. When I finally found a spot I hustled through the terminal to Spencer's gate. The flight-status monitor indicated his flight was on time. Out of breath, I politely pushed my way to the front of the crowd of greeters, just as his plane taxied up to the gate.

I checked the faces as the passengers strolled through the doorway. Visiting families and friends painted huge smiles on their faces when they'd spot their loved ones. Tired business men and women hurried off the plane, emotionless, on a mission to make a connection or to get to a meeting.

I looked at my watch. A few stragglers were deplaning, but no Spencer. I went back to check the flight arrival-monitor. I thought there must be more than one flight arriving from Sacramento. I read down the list. No, this was the only one it could be.

I approached the check-in counter. "Hi. I'm supposed to pick up a friend on this flight, but he doesn't seem to have been on it. Can you check to see if there are any messages from Spencer Davis?"

After a few phone calls, we found no evidence that Spencer made any attempt to get a message to me. Another Southwest flight from Sacramento was due to arrive in thirty minutes. I assumed he'd missed his flight and had to catch a later one.

I picked up a newspaper and leafed through the pages as I waited. More news of the *Gigabyte* was plastered all over the front page, along with more speculation into the demise of Gerald Bates. Everything pointed to the probability that he'd drowned, along with his crew. There was another quote from Morgan Johnson, the insurance investigator who'd seen the wreck firsthand, claiming the yacht broke apart. The article stated there were no immediate plans to recover the yacht; the cost would be too prohibitive, even though the boat was extremely valuable.

An announcement over the P.A. system turned my attention from the news back to the arrival of the next Southwest flight from Sacramento. Again, I anxiously watched, as a parade of travelers disembarked, but no Spencer.

I called his house. I waited, impatiently, as his answering machine went through its routine: "Hi. This is Spencer. If you're a friend, leave a message. I'll pick up if I'm home. If you're trying to sell me a subscription, credit-card protection, accidental-death insurance, or want me to change my long distance carrier, leave me your home phone number, and the hours you're most likely to be fixing dinner or watching a good movie, and I'll try to call you back."

"Spencer, it's Devonie. Are you there? I'm at the airport. Where are you?" I got no response.

I pressed the phone hook momentarily, then dialed information.

"Long Beach. I'd like an address for West Coast Insurance." I scribbled down the address. "Thank you."

I hung up the phone and glanced around the terminal at the crowds. Maybe Spencer and I had gotten our wires crossed, and he came in on a different airline. I returned to the check-in counter and asked to have him paged. Minutes passed. Nothing. Where was he? What could have happened?

It was past noon by now. I left a message for him in case he showed up, and found my way out of the terminal, back to my Jeep.

The drive back to Long Beach was not any better than when I came that morning. There didn't seem to be any good time to travel on the freeway. Horrible thoughts raced through my mind about what could have happened to Spencer, and they didn't make the trek any more endurable.

* * *

The receptionist at West Coast Insurance smiled pleasantly at me as I walked through the door.

"Is Morgan Johnson in?" I asked.

"Let me check. Your name?"

"Devonie Lace."

Morgan must have sprinted from his office to the reception area; he seemed out of breath when he greeted me.

"Devonie, what a nice surprise. Lucky you caught me here. Had a meeting with the big shots today. Usually, I'm out in the field. What can I do for you?" he asked, as he straightened his tie.

I held the envelope of photos tight in my hand. "I need to talk to you—in private, if that's possible."

"Sure. Come on back."

I followed him to an office, and he closed the door behind us as we entered. I thought back to the news reporter's interview with Morgan and his explanation for the sinking of the *Gigabyte*. He was a much better liar than me.

"I've been trying to get a hold of Clancy for a couple days. Have you seen him?" I asked.

"Clancy? No. What do you need him for?"

"I'm worried about him. You know him better than I do; is it like him to just disappear without a trace?"

"Not really. You tried his house?"

"I called. No answer."

"Hmm. Don't have a clue." Morgan fidgeted with a box of paper clips and spilled them on the desk.

I took two photos out of the envelope and shoved them in his face. "I have another question. What do you make of these?"

He analyzed them. I noticed small beads of sweat

begin to form on his forehead. He wiped them off with the back of his hand. "Where'd you get these?"

"Doesn't matter. You know what they are, don't you?" I demanded.

"Yeah." He laid the pictures on the desk.

"Why'd you say the *Gigabyte* went down because of structural damage? You and I both know she didn't break apart." I pounded my finger on one of the pictures to make my point. "Those are opened seacocks! Someone sank that yacht on purpose." My heart pounded. I'd just announced to this man, who I had no business trusting at all, that I knew way more than I should. I suddenly questioned the intelligence of this visit.

"You shouldn't have these pictures. If you're smart, you'll give them to me and forget you ever saw them." Morgan's voice was quiet and shaky—much like mine gets, just before I break down in tears.

"You're crazy if you think I'm going to forget this. There's something fishy going on, and you're obviously involved. What is it? Some sort of insurance scam? You get a percentage of the payoff if you push the claim through—no questions asked?" Beads of sweat formed on my upper lip, as the words spilled out. Composure isn't my long suit.

Morgan squeezed his eyes shut. "If it were *only* that simple. You *really* have no idea what you're getting involved in."

I decided to keep pressing. I could see in his eyes there was something he wasn't telling me. I wanted to know what it was. "Really? How about Clancy? Did he get too involved? That why he and Olive suddenly fell off the face of the earth?" My voice has risen a full octave by the end of the sentence.

"I don't know. Maybe. But if so, I didn't have anything to do with it. Clancy's a good friend. I'd never do anything to hurt him."

What does he take me for? A complete idiot? "Just tell me why you lied. What do you gain by not telling anyone why that yacht really went down?"

He placed his forehead in his palms and slowly shook his head back and forth, as he spoke. "My life."

He looked up at me. I studied his face and noticed the lines of worry etched into his forehead. I stared into his eyes, and he stared back, without looking away. I believed him.

Chapter Fifteen

It was story hour at the public library. I heard a young woman's voice reading from some classic children's book—I think it may have been *Charlotte's Web*—as I walked past the children's book section. Sitting sitting in a circle on the floor, a dozen fidgety toddlers poked and tickled each other, as the patient woman ignored their behavior and read as though she had their undivided attention.

I pulled my chair up to a computer near the back corner of the library. I entered the web address for my internet service provider and waited. The web page slowly painted itself on the screen.

I checked my e-mail, hoping Spencer had left me a message to let me know what happened. Two dozen unread messages sat in my in-box. The first one was a pretty-underwear chain letter from my friend, Beth. If it worked as planned, I would receive fifty-eight pairs of lacy underwear. What would I do with fifty-eight pairs of underpants? I deleted it.

The next fourteen were forwarded jokes. Mass delete.

The next three were from someone named Cyndi, and I only needed to read the first few lines to know Cyndi wasn't a nice girl. I'd been spammed by an Xrated solicitor. I tried to reply to the sender with a harsh message to never send me e-mail again; it came right back to me, undeliverable, of course. Delete. Delete. Delete.

I skipped over my monthly *Sunday Sailor Newsletter,* saving it in my in-box to read later.

There were no messages from Spencer, but the last entry in the list caught my attention. The sender was identified as "cwest."

Her message was flagged to send a return receipt once I'd opened it. She would know that I'd picked up the message. She requested a meeting with me. The place, date, and time would be up to me. Carissa West, the woman responsible for creating my extensive criminal history in the government's database, thought I'd be stupid enough to meet with her.

I closed her message and opened a "send message" window.

Spencer: What happened? Where are you? Are you okay? I'll keep checking my e-mail. Send me something to let me know what's happening. Devonie.

I pressed the send button, logged off of the computer, and left the library.

Why would Carissa West want to meet with me? It would surely be a setup. She'd have the entire police force waiting for me to walk into her trap. I had to find Spencer. He's the only one in the world who could clear my name.

I wasn't in the library more than thirty minutes total. I walked down the row of cars parked along the west side of the brick building I'd just exited. A green Volkswagen was parked in the spot I could have sworn I'd left my Jeep in. I walked the length of the parking lot again. No question about it. My Jeep was gone.

I emptied the contents of my purse on the bench next to the library entrance. No cell phone. I'd left it in the Jeep. I dug for change for the pay phone. I found one dime, one nickel and twenty-eight pennies.

Back inside the library, I held out the twenty-dollar bill for the woman behind the desk hoping the pathetic look on my face would arouse sympathy. "Can I get change for the phone?"

She smiled one of those smiles you get when you're sixteen and ask your mom if you can borrow the car to "run some kids over to Reno for ice cream." [Wrong.] "Oh, I'm sorry. We don't give change. There's a minimarket around the corner, about four blocks down. You can probably get change there."

It was six blocks. They wouldn't give me change unless I bought something. The pay phone took my first two quarters, wouldn't give me a dial tone, then wouldn't give me my money back. I took my remaining change and my newly-purchased pack of gum down the block to the next phone booth I found.

Jason's phone rang twelve times before I finally gave up on it. His answering machine must be on the blink again. I knew what I'd be getting him for Christmas this year.

I walked back toward Clancy's. I didn't know what to do. I didn't dare call the police to report my Jeep stolen. I used the time it took to make the long trek back to the port to think.

I stopped at another pay phone and made one more attempt to get a hold of Jason. Still no answer. I dropped in more change. This time, I got a response.

"Federal Bureau of Investigation. How may I direct your call?" came the voice, sounding very flat and uninterested.

"Dan Cooper, please."

"He's not in. Can I connect you to his voice mail?"

Voice mail—the electronic answer to call screening. Was I irritated? Yes, very. "When will he be back?"

"He's on vacation. He's due back on the fifteenth."

Oh, great. "Fifteenth? As in, two weeks from—"

"Yes. Two weeks from tomorrow. Would you like his voice mail?"

"No. Thanks." I decided against buying a lottery ticket. Didn't seem like my lucky day.

I don't know what made me decide to walk up to the front door of Clancy's office. I peered into the bucket reserved for Tex's tennis ball. It was empty. I figured someone wandered by and took it for their own pet's enjoyment. As I reached for the doorknob, something seemed strange. It wasn't closed tightly. I gave it a little shove, and it swung open.

"Clancy?" I called. No response. "Olive? Tex? Anyone here?" I cautiously stepped over the threshold of the doorway and peered inside. It was dark, but there was enough light coming through the window to allow me to see. I tiptoed over to Olive's desk. It didn't seem to look any different than usual. But, something was missing: Tex's dog blanket. It was always piled next to her desk. Now it was gone.

Why would someone take a dog blanket? I couldn't think of any explanation, unless Clancy and Olive came by. I noticed the coffee pot had been turned off and unplugged. They must have left in a hurry. The doorknob was locked, but the wooden door, swollen from the dampness, hadn't been forced tightly closed.

"What are you doing here?" came a voice from behind me.

The voice startled me, and I swung around, knocking a cup of pencils on the floor.

The dark room, and the light coming through the doorway behind the tall man, made it difficult for me to see his face.

"Wh . . . What?" I stammered.

"I said, what are you doing here?" he repeated.

I recognized the voice. I was suddenly aware of my precarious situation. This could be bad—all alone in a room with a man who obviously had something to hide. I've been told that if you're confronted by a vicious dog, the secret to survival is to appear confident and unintimidated.

"Morgan? Is that you?" I asked, with as much confidence as I could muster.

"How'd you get in here? Thought you said Clancy and Olive were gone." He reached over and switched on the lights. It *was* Morgan Johnson.

"The door wasn't closed tight. I think Clancy and Olive must have been here recently. Some of Tex's things are missing, and someone turned off the coffee pot. What are you doing here?" I could feel my heart pounding in my chest, but I kept my voice calm. If worst came to worst, I could probably outrun him, if I could get past the door.

"I got worried about them. After you came by and

told me they disappeared, I thought I ought to check it out," Morgan explained.

"They must be hiding out somewhere. You know of any place Clancy might hole up?" I asked.

"Oh, sure. There must be a hundred spots he's found while out scouting in his boat. Hidden coves on little islands. He's probably camped out right now, waiting for the dust to settle."

Dust to settle? I've heard that phrase too many times. I was getting fed up with being kept in the dark. "When's the dust going to settle? Tell me what's going on," I insisted.

"The dust will settle when the Bates Corporation people recover everything they want from the *Gigabyte*. I'm sure Clancy got a little too pushy about getting the salvage contract. Probably made someone mad. You know how he can be."

I knew he was doing his darnedest to pacify me, but I wasn't about to be pacified. Not this time. "What's the big deal about that boat? Why can't you tell anyone it was purposely sunk? Seems a lot of people would be interested in that kind of information."

Morgan pulled a chair up to Olive's desk and sat down. He seemed very tired and worn out. "A lot of people *are* interested, and they don't want it made public. If you're smart, you'll stay out of this. I don't know why the *Gigabyte* was sunk, but I know the people behind it can make sure anyone who gets in their way won't be a problem for long."

I took the seat across from Morgan. "How is it you know so much? For all I know, you could be involved up to your eyebrows."

"Two hours after I reported finding the wreck to the

Coast Guard, a couple of strong-arm types paid me a visit at home." He gingerly rubbed the back of his head and winced. "Made it perfectly clear I was mistaken about the boat not having any structural damage. They also made it clear that if I didn't support their story, I'd have some structural damage of my own to deal with."

"They threatened you?" Now I was getting somewhere.

"That's putting it mildly. Only reason they didn't kill me was because I told them I wasn't the only one who knew about the yacht. I assured them if anything happened to me, a half-dozen others would sing like birds about the *Gigabyte*. I promised to keep the whole thing under wraps until the divers recovered everything they needed."

Am I the only one who saw the absurdity here? "Then what? You know someone's eventually going to dive the wreck and expose the fact that it didn't break apart."

"I don't know. I get the feeling they hadn't thought it that far through. They were mostly concerned about the immediate recovery of whatever's on the yacht."

I remembered the photos from the *Gigabyte*. I dug them out of my purse. "Does it have anything to do with these containers stored in the hold? Look at these."

I handed Morgan the stack of pictures. He flipped through them. "I don't know. Maybe."

He handed the photos back to me. "You might think about locking these up in a safe place. The goons who came knocking on my door would love to get their hands on them. You suppose anyone knows they exist?"

Visions of the shambles I found on the *Plan C* raced through my head. I recalled how I bravely paraded through the salon, wielding my trusty baseball bat as though I could fight off any attacker. Who do I think I am? "Police Woman?" It must be the same instinct that causes a chihuahua to challenge a rottweiler. "I think someone probably does know about them: the goons who broke into my boat. Remember? This could be what they were after."

"Ordinarily, I'd say you should go to the police, but in—"

"I can't go to the police. Whoever these guys are, they've made sure of that."

"Well, I think you're probably right about Clancy. I think he's in hiding somewhere. What about you? What are you going to do?" he asked.

I didn't have a clue. The temperature felt as though it had climbed ten degrees. I wiped my damp forehead with my clammy hands and dug down deep for that confident demeanor again. "I have some friends helping me. I'll be okay."

"If you need anything, you know where to reach me. Here's my card with my office and my home numbers."

Morgan handed me a business card. I took it and slipped it in my pocket. I felt a little more able to trust him since I'd survived this confrontation without losing anything important, like blood or consciousness.

"Thanks. Should we lock the door on our way out?" I asked.

"Good idea. You ready to leave?"

"Yeah. I don't think there's anything else here of any help."

Morgan followed me out and closed the door tightly behind us. He walked back to his car, turned, and waved as he opened the door and got inside. I waved back and waited for him to drive away, before I walked down the dock to the *Little Maria.* He seemed trustworthy enough, but I still didn't want anyone to know where I was spending my nights. Visions of broken knuckles and being thrown out of a fast-moving vehicle flashed through my mind.

Chapter Sixteen

I groaned as I rolled over in my sleeping bag spread out on the floor of the *Little Maria*. Long gone were the days of youth when I could sleep all night on the hard floor at a girlfriend's slumber party and wake up without a stiff back or a painful shoulder. I would have given anything for an air mattress or even a pillow. I rolled up in a ball on my knees and moaned some more as I crawled out of the warm bag, shivering in the cold air.

"Brrr. It's colder than a beaver's belly in here." I rolled up the sleeping bag and tossed it in the corner.

My stomach growled and I thought about where my next meal would come from. I still had some of the money Spencer lent me. I decided to treat myself and walk down to the little restaurant on the corner. They've got a veggie omelet that's to die for.

As I laced up my shoes, I thought I heard a strange noise outside. I stopped and listened. Nothing. I continued with the other shoe. There it was again. An intermittent squawk, like a radio. I stood up straight and cocked my head to get a better listen. There was definitely something going on outside.

I climbed up the steps and peeked over the railing toward Clancy's office. Five police cars were parked around the little shack, blocking any passage in or out. Uniformed policemen milled around, obviously looking for something. Two men worked on getting the front door open, while others snooped around, peering in the windows and looking under tarps and canvas sails piled on the porch.

There was one other boat tied up next to the *Little Maria*. It was a smaller fishing boat, but it could have easily given the larger boat a run for her money. I quietly climbed over the railing onto the dock, checking over my shoulder to make sure no one was paying any attention to my activities. I stepped onto the other boat and hurried into the main cabin. The keys were dangling from the ignition. What is it with these fishermen? They've never heard of boat thieves? I pulled the keys from the ignition and tossed them out into the water as I made my way back to the *Little Maria*.

I released the line holding the stern to the dock. I snuck to the bow of the *Little Maria* and untied the last line preventing my escape. I grabbed an old oar laying on the deck and shoved the boat away from the dock. The boat drifted a little, then sat motionless just a few feet from solid ground. I tiptoed back to the pilot seat and started the engine.

The sound of the diesel caught the attention of several police officers wandering around Clancy's office.

"Hey! There's someone on that boat!" one of them yelled, pointing in my direction.

I shoved the lever full throttle ahead, and the *Little Maria* lunged forward. I turned the wheel sharply, and away we went. On the run, again. I looked back to see the small army of policemen racing down the dock. As I expected, they immediately jumped onto the other boat at the dock. I glanced back to see their frustration at not finding the keys. They waved their arms, stamped their feet, and watched helplessly, as my wake grew longer—measuring the distance between us.

I motored past the mouth of the harbor and headed southwest along the coastline, keeping fairly close to the shore. The morning fog was light and already lifting. I eased back on the throttle and watched the shore. I tried to remember the boat landings I'd seen along this section of coastline.

I decided to just hang off the shoreline for a while—to think. I didn't know what my next move should be. What were those policemen looking for? Me? Did Morgan tell them I was there?

The sun burned off the little bit of fog, and its warmth felt good on my back. I forgot how cold I had been this morning, but I couldn't forget how hungry I was. I remembered I had a couple of apples and a banana stashed in a bag down below deck. I reached for the throttle to stop the boat, when I noticed the annoying sound heading my direction. I spun around and scanned the horizon.

A helicopter. For the first time ever, I cursed the sunshine for chasing the fog away. It wasn't far off, and there'd be no outrunning it. Still, I shoved the throttle forward and turned toward the coast. I was about a mile from shore. The helicopter gained on the *Little Maria* quickly. The next sound I heard made me feel sick to my stomach: the boat's diesel engine sputtered and coughed as it swallowed its last ounce of fuel before it quit.

"No," I said, staring at the fuel gauge. "Please, don't

be out of fuel," I begged. I turned the key and listened to the engine crank, but with no success. "Please, please, please . . ." I pleaded. I lost.

I jumped out of the pilot seat and hurried below deck. The helicopter couldn't land on the boat. They could only keep me in sight and radio my position to another boat. I was sure that's what they were doing.

I found a plastic zip-lock bag with the crumbs of some potato chips still inside. I dumped the contents of my purse on the floor, dropped to my knees, and picked out what I determined to be most important. I put all my cash, except for the pennies, into the plastic bag. Then I slipped the photos of the *Gigabyte* in. I dropped the keys from the trunk in and zipped it up tight. I slipped the small package into the waistband of my pants and rushed to the tank racks.

I checked the gauges on the remaining scuba tanks. I picked the fullest one and hoisted it on my back. I grabbed a mask and flippers and struggled to get back up to the deck. Adrenaline gave me the strength I needed to haul my body, plus all that equipment, up the steps. On deck, I reached down and removed my shoes. I tied the laces together and then to one of my belt loops. I slipped the mask on my face, dropped the fins over the side, and jumped in.

Nearly a mile off shore, I'd be swimming for a long time. I surfaced only as often as necessary, to verify my position. I decided on a direct route to the shore for the shortest swim. That's probably exactly what my pursuers expected, but I wasn't too keen on becoming shark food, either.

As I got closer to the beach, I headed for a pier that looked promising for giving me some cover. When I finally reached it, I clung to a barnacle-covered post and rested for a few minutes. I liberated myself from the scuba equipment and let the ocean have it. I stayed under the pier, as I made my way to the beach, careful not to get tangled in anyone's fishing line.

I crawled through the wet sand, then out from under the shade of the huge wooden structure into the sunshine. I laid there and let the sun work at drying my soaked clothes. After a while, I struggled to get my feet into the wet tennis shoes, but the sand wouldn't cooperate. I walked to the water and rinsed all the sand off, then shoved my feet into the wet shoes.

A day like this would normally bring droves of people to the beach if it had been a weekend. Since it was midweek, the crowds were thin. I didn't see any policemen roaming around, but I thought I'd better not make like a sitting duck, and find some dark, inconspicuous place to hide out.

First, I had to try to contact the cavalry. I jogged up the steps of the pier and went straight for the first restaurant I came to. I brushed the sand off and walked inside.

A bushy-haired, blond surfer-type was using the phone when I got inside. I could hear his frustrated, impatient voice barking into the telephone. "The surf's awesome today! What difference does it make if I'm home for lunch!?" He was apparently having an argument with his mother.

I sat down on a bench near the front door and waited my turn. Someone had left today's paper sitting next to me. I picked it up and leafed through it.

The headlines were the same ones I'd been reading for the last several months: *Iraq ousted more U.N.*

weapons inspectors. Threats were being made. Troops were being deployed. Missiles were being aimed. Rumors of Iraqi chemical warfare were circulating.

After reading the Iraq story, I found the horoscope section. "It may seem as though the world is against you right now. Be patient. This, too, shall pass."

What? I read it, again. Whatever happened to those happy little horoscopes I remembered reading as a kid? The ones that hinted at the promise of new love, or the rekindling of an old love? Or the possibility of wealth and good fortune? Who wants to be hit in the face with a forecast that borders on depressing?

I folded the paper and laid it back down on the seat next to me. Mr. Beach Boy continued his sparring with the object of his frustration on the other end of the phone line. He waved his free hand in the air, then clenched his fist and emulated punching something, or someone. "I'll be home by six! Don't rent my room to Bernie!" Then he slammed the phone down and stormed out of the restaurant.

I approached the phone as I pulled the plastic ziplock bag from my pants and fished out enough change to make the call.

"Please be there," I whispered, as I counted the rings echoing in my ear.

"Hello?" came the voice over the phone.

"Jason? You're home!" Hallelujah. I couldn't believe my ears.

"Dev?"

"Oh, Jason. Am I ever glad to hear your voice."

"Gee, thanks. What's the matter? You okay?"

"No. I need you to come and get me. My Jeep was stolen. The police are catching up to me, and the *Little*

Maria conked out a mile from shore." The words spilled out of my mouth in a steady, nervous stream.

"What? Little what? What are you talking about?"

"I'll fill you in when you get here. I'm in Huntington Beach at a pier. I don't know the name, but—" I turned to see a pair of uniforms standing in the front doorway. I estimated the length of the phone cord, and pulled it with me, as I slipped around the corner. It just barely reached. "Listen, Jason. Wait a minute," I whispered. I peeked around the corner. The two policemen were being escorted through some doors, I presumed to the kitchen to conduct a search. I set the phone down, then quickly slipped to my previous seat and picked up the newspaper. I hurried back around the corner and searched for the entertainment section. I opened it up to the movie section. "Ah. Here it is." I put the phone back to my ear. "Get here as fast as you can. I'll meet you at the Pierside Cinemas in Huntington Beach. It's right on the Pacific Coast Highway."

"Cinema? What are we going to see?"

"*The Killing of Devonie Lace,* if you don't get here right away."

"Okay, okay. I get the picture. How will I find you?"

"*Cinderella* is playing. I'll be in the back row."

"Okay. I'll get there as fast as I can. Be careful."

"Thanks, Jason. You, too."

I stepped around the corner to hang up the phone. The two cops pushed through the swinging doors and headed my direction. I did an about-face and marched back down the hall to the restrooms. The obvious choice would be the door with the figure wearing a skirt. That's probably exactly the room they'd search. I pushed through the other door. A man, washing his hands at the sink, glanced up at me, surprised. He looked around the otherwise empty lavatory, ready to correct my mistake.

I took the upper hand. "Uh, oh. You're in the wrong one," I said, smiling.

His face turned red. "I am? I could've sworn—"

"It's okay. I won't tell," I promised.

He quickly dried his hands and rushed out. I watched as he inspected the sign on the door. He turned and looked at me. "*You're* in the wrong one, not me," he corrected.

"You're kidding. Really? Well, I wasn't gonna tell on you. Don't tell on me. Okay?"

He shook his head as he backed out of the doorway. "Okay."

A high window leading outside looked promising. I dragged the large trash can to the wall under it and climbed up. It would only open a few inches. Scrap that idea. I could hide in one of the two stalls, but if they came in searching, I'd literally be a sitting duck. I moved the trash can back to its original position. It was big enough, and it was nearly empty. It would have to do. I lifted the swinging lid off and climbed inside, lowering the lid back in place over my head. I listened, as the squeaky door swung open.

"Yeah. She was right in here, officers. Plain as day. Tried to tell me *I* was in the wrong one. Bet she's the one you're looking for." Little weasel. I should've known he'd squeal.

I heard the heavy footsteps of three or four men walking around the small room. They banged the stall doors against the walls as they pushed them open. I held my breath and felt a drop of sweat roll down the side of my face. I didn't dare move to wipe it off, or I'd make a sound and give away my hiding place.

"Well, she's not here now. She must have slipped out while we weren't looking."

"What'd she do, officers? She didn't look danger-ous," the weasel asked.

I never heard their reply. They dashed out after as-suming I was gone. I lifted the lid slightly and peeked out. The coast was clear. I climbed back out of the can and slipped out through the door. The officers were outside, interviewing passersby. I tiptoed down the hall and through the swinging doors into the kitchen. I raced through a doorway leading outside.

I stopped briefly to get my bearings: the ocean to my left, dry land to my right. I jogged down the wooden pier to the sidewalk. I disappeared into a group of tourists and stayed with them until we all reached the highway. A small mom-and-pop grocery store with an open door offered a momentary hiding place. I stepped inside and walked up to the counter.

"Can you tell me how to get to the Pierside Cine-mas?" I asked the old Oriental man behind the counter. Boy, was he old. He must have been a hundred, if he was a day. There were more wrinkles on his face than in a whole bag of prunes.

"Sure. Two blocks, that way." The man pointed his bony finger toward the window, behind me. "Can't miss it."

"Thanks," I said, rushing back out the door.

I bought my ticket, a bag of unbuttered popcorn, and settled into a seat at the back of the theater. I'd come in just as the wicked stepmother locked poor Cinderella up to prevent her from going to the ball. My popcorn was completely gone before the glass slipper came off and caused all that commotion.

Chapter Seventeen

"**I** thought you were opposed to let's see how do you put it? 'Promoting unfulfilled fantasies that can only lead to disappointments due to unrealistic expectations by exposing young minds to senseless fairytales,' " a voice whispered. Jason reached into my empty popcorn container.

"Jason! You made it," I gasped. He couldn't possibly know how glad I was to see him.

"Ready to get out of here?" he asked.

Cinderella was halfway through its second showing, and although I'd seen the ending once already, I wanted to see it again. "Not yet," I whispered.

Though I couldn't see it in the dark, I sensed the grin on his face. "Okay. I'm going for popcorn. You want anything?" he offered.

"No. Thanks."

"Okay, what the heck's going on now?" Jason badgered me as we left the theater.

"I'll tell you on the way. Come on," I ordered, grabbing his arm and leading him to the parking lot. As we approached Jason's pickup, I made a conscious effort to reach the driver-side door first.

"Mind if I—"

"No. I'm driving," he stated, emphatically.

"But—"

"I'm driving. End of discussion," he blurted.

"Fine. I may as well sit on the roof, so I can wave to the crowd," I complained.

"What?"

Right. Like he doesn't know he drives slower than a ninety-eight-year-old man looking for an ice-cream parlor on the wrong side of the street. "You drive so slow, it feels like we're in a parade," I reminded him.

"Do I have to remind you that at eighty-miles-per-hour, you're no longer steering, you're aiming?"

Gee, where had I heard that before? Oh, yeah—from Jason—a million times before. Make that a million and one. "And at fifty-five miles-per-hour, you're crawling on the freeway, while a bazillion other drivers pass you like a turtle in the middle of a rabbit stampede."

"Ah. The old tortoise and hare analogy. You remember how that story goes, don't you?" he pointed out.

I didn't have the energy to argue. I was tired and beat. "Fine. You drive. Wake me up when we get there."

"Where are we going, if you don't mind me asking?"

"I think Los Angeles would be a good place to get lost for a while. Let's find a public library. I want to see if Spencer has answered my e-mail."

Jason put the pickup in gear. "Los Angeles, it is—but you're not going to sleep, young lady." Then, he broke into his best Ricky Ricardo impression. "You got some 'splainin' to do, Lucy."

*   *   *

My shoulders slumped with disappointment as I read down the messages in my in-box. Nothing from Spencer. My worry was quickly turning to fear. Had I gotten Spencer into terrible trouble?

I turned to Jason, sitting next to me, paging through the sports section of the *Los Angeles Times*. "You still have that old Motorola cell phone?" I asked.

"Yeah. Why?"

"Have it with you?"

"In the truck. Want me to get it?"

"No. Not yet. Let me see the entertainment section of that paper."

I searched through the pages until I found the name and address of a popular local restaurant. I began a new message, addressed to Carissa West.

Meet me at the Outback Steakhouse near your office—tonight at 7. Devonie

Lace.

I scheduled the message to be sent in twenty minutes. Jason reached for my hand and took it off the mouse.

"What are you doing? Didn't you tell me she's the one setting you up? You can't meet her. It's a trap," he warned.

"I know. I have a plan. Let's go. We've only got twenty minutes."

We found a parking spot on the street in front of the U.S. Justice Department building. It was late afternoon and the sun beat through the passenger window with magnified force. While Jason fed the parking meter, I fanned my face with a map and rummaged through his glove box, searching for a small screwdriver. Nothing. How can an appliance repairman not carry a simple screwdriver in his truck? I checked my watch; time was running out. Jason slid back into the driver seat.

"Don't you have a screwdriver?" I asked.

"Back at the shop, in my toolbox."

"Geez. What if you broke down? What would you do?" I nagged.

"I'd call a tow truck. What do you need a screwdriver for?"

I ignored his question. I had a sudden stroke of genius. "The gum!" I grabbed my purse and dumped it out on the seat, looking for the pack of chewing gum I was forced to buy in order to get change for the phone. I used a short strip of tinfoil from the gum wrapper to enhance the capabilities of Jason's old cell phone. He watched me, curiously, as I worked on the device.

"What are you doing?" he asked.

"I'm turning your phone into a scanner."

"Where'd you learn to do that?"

I recalled a rainy afternoon about three years ago, when Spencer and I worked together in the same office. Things were kind of slow that day, and Spencer was bored. I'd watched him fiddle with a cell phone and asked him what he was up to. He was a snooper—not malicious, just nosy. He was listening to a cell phone conversation going on between our manager and some woman, obviously not his wife. Spencer's knowledge of that conversation kept him employed with San Tel longer than he probably should have been. When he finally stepped over the line and modified some of his friend's credit card records to reduce their debt, even our unfaithful manager couldn't save his hide. "Spencer showed me how, back when we worked for San Tel. Only works for listening to calls on analog phones, but we may get lucky."

"Who are you going to listen to?"

"Carissa West works here. I'm betting my best pony she'll get on her phone when she receives my e-mail message."

"What if she doesn't use her cell phone?"

Another important bit of information I learned from Spencer is that government agencies are not very trusting, even of their own employees. He described some of the listening devices being "tested" in the State building, where he eventually gained honest employment. "The call she's likely to make, she won't want any federal *ears* listening in on. The government's notorious for spying on their employees at work. I bet there are more bugs on the phones in those offices than the Watergate Hotel ever saw." I nodded toward the glass windows of the office building across the street from us. I completed the task of modifying Jason's phone and checked my watch.

"There. Mission accomplished. She should be getting the e-mail message right about now."

I held the phone to my ear and scanned through the channels, listening to any cell phone conversations taking place in the area.

"What do you hear?"

"Shh." I held my finger to my lips.

Jason watched my face for any expression. He

looked like an obedient dog, waiting for his master to release him from the "stay command," so he could eat the dog cookie placed on his nose.

I scanned through the channels, stopping whenever I heard a promising conversation. "If Carissa is at her desk, she should have received my e-mail message about three minutes ago. That should be enough time," I murmured to Jason; my mind focused on the scanner, my eyes on the building.

My intuition told me to hold on the conversation I'd just landed on. A woman's voice opened the dialogue:

"It's me. She wants to meet."

A man replied. His gravely voice overpowered her squeak. "When?" he asked.

"Tonight. Seven. You think she's made the connection between Bates and Aziz?"

"Doesn't matter if she has. You notify all the forces?" the gruff voice responded.

"Not yet. I just got the message. Are we sticking with the original plan?"

I sat, biting my lip, as I listened to the two of them plan my demise. I knew I was in trouble. These people had connections and skills that could keep me in hiding indefinitely. I fanned my face again. The sun seemed to be burning right through my skin.

"Yes. Bring her in." His order reminded me of a general sending his troops into battle.

"It's as good as done. I'll call you after," she promised.

The connection closed and I dropped the phone in my lap.

"What? What? Tell me what you heard?!" Jason

demanded. He could tell by the pasty color my face had turned, that there was trouble at Black Rock.

I barely heard Jason's pleading, as I ran the conversation back through my head. Finally, Jason grabbed the collar of my shirt and pulled my face up to his.

"Tell me what you heard, or I'll . . . I'll . . . take off my shoes. I have ways of making you talk."

"Oh, God. No. Not that."

"Talk to me, girl," he gritted, still holding my collar.

"You ever hear of Mohammed Aziz? He's an oil industrialist."

Jason pondered for a moment. "No. Don't think so. What's he got to do with this?"

"I don't know, but there's a connection between him and Bates. Let's get back to the library. I'll explain on the way."

I searched for any document I could find with both Gerald Bates and Mohammed Aziz names in it. From all accounts, Gerald Bates had just returned from a business meeting with Mohammed Aziz the evening before he set sail on the *Gigabyte,* never to be seen again. The stories claimed he called ahead from the San Francisco Airport to his office, to have the yacht stocked and ready to sail early the next morning. He apparently scheduled a last-minute vacation cruise to the Hawaiian Islands and wanted his crew prepared.

I nudged Jason with my elbow. "Have you seen any reference to where the *Gigabyte* was berthed in San Francisco?"

"No. Think your uncle might know?"

"He probably would, but he's in Europe right now.

George might know. Come on. Let's go," I said, as I jumped out of my seat and hustled toward the exit.

Jason hurried to catch up with me. "Who's George?"

"One of Uncle Doug's salesmen. Come on. Hurry."

We climbed back into Jason's pickup, and I punched the number for Lace Marina into the cell phone as we sat in Jason's pickup, parked in front of the library.

"Lace Marina. This is George," came the voice through the phone.

"George. It's Devonie."

"Devonie! How are you?"

"I'm okay, George. Okay? Listen—"

"I haven't seen you for ages! When are you going to come by and visit us?"

"Soon, George. Listen, I need—"

"Your uncle said you've been sailing around the Caribbean for a few months. I bet that must have been a great trip."

I rolled my eyes, shook my head, and slid four inches down Jason's bench seat. Half the police force was out to take me down, I felt like I was sinking in quicksand, and George wanted to make small talk. "It was, George. But, I need—"

"Did you take any pictures? I love pictures."

I clenched my teeth. "George! Yes, I took pictures. You can have them all, but please let me finish a sentence."

"Oh. Sorry. What's up?"

I felt like I'd just kicked Lassie. "Thanks, George. Sorry I'm so cranky, but I need your help. Would you happen to know where in San Francisco the *Gigabyte* was berthed? That's Gerald Bates's yacht—the one that was lost."

"Right. It was lost, but now it's found; so I've heard."

"That's the one. I remember Uncle Doug talking about the guy who owns the marina where it was berthed. Do you know who that was?"

"Aw, heck, yeah! That's old Hugo Baumgartner. We call him Captain Huey. Great guy. You should've seen him dance on the tables at Scoma's at that convention we went to last year. Had us all rolling on the floor."

"That's great, George. Do you know the name of the marina?"

"Better than that. I can give you his number. I've got it right here. Let's see. I've got it somewhere in this crazy thing. Now, where is that number."

George hummed into the phone. I could picture him sitting at his desk as he searched through the huge rolodex file on his desk. "Ah! Here it is! Got a pen?"

I recorded the number as George recited it to me.

"Thanks, George. I'll bring those pictures by just as soon as I get a chance."

"Can't wait. Any shots of island natives in bikinis?"

"Just male ones, George. You know it was me behind the lens."

"Oh. Well, I'd like to see them anyway. You come see us soon."

"I will. Bye."

Jason had rolled the windows down in his pickup while I talked with George. The sidewalks were growing busy with passing pedestrians out to grab a bite to eat, or catch a movie. The scent of a pepperoni pizza wafted into the pickup as a red-haired, freckle-faced pizza delivery boy waltzed by. Jason watched intently until the blue, red, and craft-brown cardboard container disappeared around the corner.

"You hungry?" he asked, almost drooling.

"You know, I'm starving. Can we find a place with a salad bar?"

"You kidding? If we can't find a salad bar in L.A., then we must be idiots."

"Okay. Your mission, Mr. Walters, should you agree to accept it, is to find a place to eat where both you and I will be happy. In the meantime, I'll put a call through to Captain Huey."

"Captain Huey?" Jason questioned.

"Yeah. He owns the marina where the *Gigabyte* was kept."

Jason drove while I punched in the numbers. Someone picked up on the third ring.

"Bay Marina," the raspy male voice announced.

"Is Hugo in?" I asked.

"Huey? Yeah. Hang on. He's out cleaning a fish or something."

I could hear the man yelling outside for Huey to drop that fish and come to the phone. I could also hear Jason chanting, "Salad bar . . . chili dogs. . . . Come to Papa," as he drove around the busy streets of L.A. with no idea where he was going.

"Yeah. This is Huey," the abrupt voice blurted into my ear.

"Hello, Huey. My name's Devonie Lace. Doug Lace is my uncle."

"Doug? Sure! How the heck is that old far—codger?"

"He's having a ball somewhere in Europe right now. I wonder if you can . . . I sort of got myself in a . . . well . . . I need some help. I wonder if you can—"

"You name it," Huey broke in, before I could finish.

Thank God for blind cooperation. Some days, everything I touch turns into a new experience in resistance. This man didn't know me from Adam—or, rather, Eve—and here he was, offering help. "I understand Gerald Bates's yacht, the *Gigabyte,* used to be kept at your marina?"

"That's right."

"Were you at the marina the morning Gerald Bates left for the Hawaiian Islands?"

"I was here. I'm here just about every day."

"Do you remember seeing Bates?" I asked.

"No. Never saw him."

"Did he leave before you arrived?"

"Nope. Said *I* was here. The *Gigabyte* wasn't. Hadn't been here for about a week. I figured they took it out to sea—big storm that night. *El Nino,* you know. Whole California coast was beat by that storm."

My mind raced in circles as it tried to piece together what it had just learned. "So I heard. Huh. So you never actually saw Gerald Bates that day?"

"Nope," he confirmed.

"Well, thanks, Huey. You've been a big help."

Jason's eyes lit up with excitement. "There! Victory!" he announced, pointing to the sign on the restaurant. "Joe's Jungle—where carnivores and herbivores can meet and eat."

I ordered a Southwest Grilled Chicken Salad, with the dressing on the side. Jason ordered prime rib with lots of horseradish sauce and extra butter and sour cream for his potato. I sipped my water, trying to keep the lemon slice at bay, while I watched Jason guzzle a glass of Diet Coke he'd poured from a can.

"You know the sweetener in that stuff'll kill you, don't you?" I commented. I knew it was a useless effort to try to talk nutrition with Jason, but I always have to try. "And drinking out of aluminum cans is eventually going to cause the end of our civilization, just like the fall of Rome," I continued.

"How do you figure?"

"Rome fell because all the people were brain damaged from lead poisoning," I explained.

"I'm sure I'm going to be sorry I asked, but how did that happen?"

"It was the lead from the pewter cups they drank out of, and the plates they ate off of, and the pots they cooked in. They were just pumped full of it. Who knows what kind of damage you're doing to your body eating and drinking the way you do," I lectured.

He squinted at me with his skeptical green eyes. "According to you, everything I eat's gonna kill me. Tell you what: I'll keep eating this way, and if I die, you can say you told me so."

"Go ahead. Make jokes. Go through life fat, dumb, and happy."

"I will. Now, can we change the subject?" Jason had reached his exasperation threshold. I knew it was time to stop with the nutrition police work.

"Good idea. What about the *Gigabyte?* According to the story in the *Chronicle,* Bates should have boarded it on November fifteenth. I can't find anyone who actually saw him or the yacht on that day."

"He could have been shuttled out to the yacht on a small boat. Why is this bothering you?"

If I were a character in a comic strip, a light bulb would have flashed over my head at that moment. "Wait. That's it. November fifteenth doesn't fit."

"What? What's wrong with the fifteenth?" Jason asked.

"It can't be. The *Gigabyte* was already on the bottom on the fifteenth." I settled back in the booth as the realization hit me.

"How do you know?" Jason queried.

"Because Roy Hastings recorded the date he found the wreck on his GPS. I remember reading it. It was November tenth. That was the last entry. Bates couldn't have boarded the *Gigabyte* on the fifteenth. It was already sunk."

"You sure? You could have the date wrong."

How soon they forget. I've explained to Jason a hundred times; if my last name were Right, my first name would be Always—at least when it comes to remembering dates and numbers. I glared at him. "You're birthday is March fourteenth, I graduated from college on June ninth, I was hired at San Tel on August twelfth, I quit San Tel on October eleventh, your sister's birthday is—"

"Okay, okay. I get the picture. So the yacht sunk on the tenth. What does it mean?"

"It means someone made up the story about Bates returning to San Francisco on that date. I bet he wasn't anywhere near the city. He wasn't on his yacht. He was somewhere in the Middle East when the *Gigabyte* went down."

"So where is he now? How could he just vanish?"

"I bet he had help. Someone went to a lot of trouble to make it look like he'd returned."

Chapter Eighteen

I tapped my fingers on Jason's kitchen table as I counted the rings over the telephone stuck to my ear. Four rings; then, "Federal Bureau of Investigation. How may I direct your call?"

I sat up in the chair. "Dan Cooper, please."

"Mr. Cooper's on vacation—"

"I know. Voice mail will be fine."

I listened to agent Cooper's generic, almost bland greeting: "This is agent Cooper. I'm out of the office until the fifteenth. Leave me a message."

I cleared my throat. "Dan, this is Devonie Lace. You won't believe it, but I'm in trouble, again. I can't tell you where I am or how to reach me. I hope you're one of those insane people who checks his messages daily, even on vacation. I'll keep checking with your office." I hung up the phone and turned to see Jason searching the refrigerator.

"How much room do you have on your credit card?" I asked as I stood up and began pacing the floor.

"Huh?" he responded, still rifling through the vegetable crisper—where he stores his candy bars.

"Enough to get two round-trip tickets to San Francisco?" I asked.

"Bus?"

"Please, no! Plane tickets. Southwest. They're cheap."

"What've you got in mind?" He finally turned to look at me, while unwrapping a Mars Bar.

"I *have* to find Spencer. I just know Stan Parker is involved somehow."

Jason downed the candy bar in two bites, then reached back in the fridge and pulled a hotdog out of its plastic package and jammed the entire thing in his mouth. "You're not thinking of trying any of that Rambo stuff, are you?" he asked, his mouth still full.

I laughed. "Me? No way."

"Good."

"That's why I'm bringing you along."

Jason choked on his hotdog. He coughed and wagged his finger at me, unable to speak.

"Don't worry. I'm just kidding," I assured him, checking the size of my nose one more time.

He patted his chest and swallowed the half-chewed wiener.

I gathered up my purse and headed for the door. "Come on. We'll need your cell phone."

The next Southwest flight to San Francisco was scheduled to leave in just a little over an hour. Jason and I made our way down the long corridors, through the security stop, and to our gate just in time to hear the boarding call. We obtained our boarding passes and, luckily, found two empty seats next to each other. Someone had left a newspaper in the seat pocket in front of me. I snatched it up and leafed through the pages, looking for any *Gigabyte* updates.

I wanted to check my messages before the seatbelt sign came on. I nudged Jason. "Let me see your phone."

He was half asleep. "Huh? Oh. Okay." He dug it out of his pocket. "Here you go."

I called my number and waited for my answering machine to pick up. As soon as I heard my voice on the recording, I punched in my secret code and listened to my messages. The first one was from Craig.

"Devonie, are you there? Please pick up. Where are you? I've been trying to reach you for days. Please call me. I'll be home tomorrow."

I squeezed my eyes shut and rubbed my forehead. I knew I should call him, but I didn't know what I was going to say to him yet. I shoved that worry to the back of my mind.

I heard a click, then some static, then a brief silence. The voice was barely audible, just a whisper. I could make out the first word: "Devonie." I couldn't be sure about the rest of the message. It sounded like a frantic, "Oh man, they're here," then the line went dead. I powered the phone off and handed it back to Jason. The voice could have been Spencer's, but I wasn't sure. The knot in my stomach grew larger and tenser with each passing minute. By the end of the ninety-minute flight, the imprint of my fingernails was carved into my palms.

The girl at the car-rental counter pointed through the glass windows at a bright-purple, Plymouth Neon parked out front. I gaped at it. "No. We can't take that car," I blurted. "We need something a little less . . . uh . . . something more . . . inconspicuous."

She gazed out the window at the collection of brightly colored cars. "We have a yellow one."

I smiled at her. "White? Do you have white?"

She frowned. "Not in an economy car. We have a white Taurus, but it costs more."

"We'll take it," I blurted.

Jason elbowed me. "Wait a minute! How much more?" he asked as I took him by the arm and pulled him away from the counter, out of earshot of the car-rental agent.

"I'll pay you back, when this is over. We can't be prancing around the Silicon Valley in that . . . that . . . Mickey Mouse car. We'll stand out like a . . . like a rodeo clown at a polo match."

Jason slumped his shoulders and trudged back to the counter. "I guess we'll take the Taurus."

Silicon Valley, an area about twenty-five miles long, ten miles wide, and approximately forty-five miles southeast of San Francisco, is home to some of the wealthiest high-tech companies in the world. Countless entrepreneurs hitched their wagons to that fortune-bound horse called "technology," and Gerald Bates was one of the visionaries who had the stamina, fortitude, intelligence, and incredible good luck to come out on top. Employees of these companies enjoy the monetary rewards of working for a veritable gold mine.

As Jason and I sat in our plain white Taurus in the parking lot of the Bates Building, we glanced around at the other cars parked there. I counted one Ferrari, one Porsche, two Jaguars, six Mercedeses and twice as many BMW's. Our Ford was painfully out of place—much as I wanted to be inconspicuous.

Jason sat behind the wheel and drooled over the expensive sports cars surrounding us. I nudged his shoulder. "Trade places."

"What?" he hissed, as he squinted at me through those green eyes. The last time I saw a face like that, Clint Eastwood was on the big screen, asking some punk if he felt lucky. I'm not easily intimidated by Jason's attempts at being tough.

"You heard me. I want to drive," I replied.

He sneered at me. "Uh uh. No way. I want to live to use my return ticket to San Diego."

"Come on. I'm not gonna do anything crazy. I just don't want to lose this guy."

"I've seen *Bullet*. You'll have us airborne over the streets of San Francisco," Jason argued.

"Sissy!"

"Go ahead. Insult me. That's why you're so successful at winning friends and influencing people."

"Okay, fine." I turned back and crossed my arms over my chest. "You can drive, but you have to swear you'll stick to him, no matter what. Spencer's life may depend on this."

"Have faith. I won't let you down."

I gave Jason a skeptical glance. "Right. Let me see your phone."

I powered on Jason's cell phone and ran the script through my head one more time. I punched in the number for Bates Corporation and impatiently navigated my way through the electronic maze designed to direct my call as quickly and efficiently as possible without human contact. After repeating the sequence three times, being disconnected twice, and misselecting two options, I finally reached the voice mail for Stan Parker. In exasperation, I pressed the zero button and waited for a human being to come on the line.

"Hello. I need to speak to Stan Parker right away. It's an emergency. Can you please page him? I'll wait."

The operator paused briefly. "The nature of the emergency?"

I rolled my eyes. "A personal emergency. Please!"

"Hold please." A flood of elevator music streamed into my ear, causing the opposite reaction than was intended. I checked my watch. Five minutes later, the operator came back on the line. "I'm sorry. I can't seem to locate Mr. Parker. I can put you through to his voice mail."

"No. Already tried that. Page him again. Tell him it's Carissa West."

She didn't reply. She shoved me back into the flood of elevator music. I waited again.

Jason ogled a burgundy Jaguar parked opposite us. He looked like a kid paging through the J. C. Penny's Christmas catalog.

Finally, a man's voice barked into my ear. "Stan Parker. Carissa?"

I cleared my throat. "No, Mr. Parker. It's Spencer Davis's assistant. I'm calling to see how you're coming with those flow charts."

He was silent for a moment. "Flow charts? But Maggie said you were—"

"Carissa West? Yes, I know. I had to get your attention." My heart was racing, but not as fast as my brain trying to stay one step ahead of Mr. Stan Parker.

"Who is this?" he demanded.

"Not until you tell me where Spencer Davis is."

"What? How the heck should I know where he is?"

"Come on, Stan. You and I both know you're not the network administrator for Bates Corporation. People are missing, and I think you know where they are," I accused. The high pitch and shakiness of my voice gave away my nervousness.

"You're crazy. I don't know what your—"

"Oh, really? I'll show you just how crazy I am. I know for a fact that Gerald Bates wasn't on the *Gigabyte* when it went down. I know it was deliberately sunk—someone opened the seacocks. I have pictures to prove it. I also know that on the day it sank, Bates was in Baghdad, meeting with Mohammed Aziz. Am I warm, Mr. Parker?" I figured as long as I was going out on a limb, I may as well start with hard facts.

"You don't know anything. Some kind of kook." His voice took on an arrogant tone. I had to call his bluff.

"Kook? Then why haven't you hung up on me? If you weren't interested in what I had to say, you would have blown me off before I finished my first sentence."

"Who are you?!"

"I told you, not until you tell me where Spencer Davis is. If you don't, I'm going to the FBI with everything I know." I was hoping I wouldn't have to play all my cards, but this guy wouldn't budge.

"They'll laugh you out of their office. No, better, they'll lock you up in the state hospital. Little men in white jackets ... I'm sure your familiar," Parker insulted.

My voice grew steadier. "Yeah, Stan. How about

this? I know about Harlan and Carissa West. I know about Kent Morrison. I know about Roy Hastings." I grasped for my last cards. "I even know about Clancy and Olive McGreggor. I know it all, *Mr. Parker.*"

"What do you know about—"

Out of cards, I played the joker. "And Texaco! I know about Texaco."

"You don't know anything. You're crazy." Click. The line went dead.

I guess I went far enough. If I'd played my cards right, Mr. Parker would be on the run—just where I wanted him. I powered off the cell phone and handed it back to Jason. "You ready to rumble? I expect we'll see Mr. Parker through those doors any second now."

Jason turned the key in the ignition. "You better hope he's not the owner of that Ferrari, or we'll be in trouble."

"Only if he knows we're following him. Just be cool."

Thirty seconds later, Stan Parker blasted through the glass doors and raced to his car, a silver-blue Toyota minivan. Jason let out a sigh of relief, as he put the Taurus in gear and pulled out of our spot. We eased out of the parking lot and followed the minivan south onto the freeway. Jason kept one car between us and Parker to avoid being spotted. Luckily, Stan Parker used his turn signals faithfully; so we were never surprised by his moves. We exited the freeway after about ten miles and headed east toward the foothills. We followed him into a rural subdivision, called "Iron Horse Estates." Jason stayed back far enough to avoid attention, but close enough that we could always keep him in sight if he turned a corner.

The minivan finally pulled into a long circular driveway in front of a large ranch-style home. The red tile roof shaded two ferns hanging in the Spanish arches on each side of the entry. A perfectly manicured lawn led to a flower bed bursting with begonias, impatiens, and oxalis. The flowing branches of a weeping-willow tree swayed with the breeze. The pleasantness of the scene momentarily distracted me from the seriousness of the situation.

"Stop right here," I instructed Jason. We parked on the street and watched as Stan Parker climbed out of the minivan.

A golden retriever, with a red bandana tied around his neck, barreled around the corner of the house to greet him. Pink flowers and dirt clods flew through the air as the big dog tore through the flower bed. Stan Parker covered his eyes with his hands and shook his head.

"That's Tex!" I blurted, pointing at the bumbling beast.

Jason grabbed my hand and pulled it down. "Don't get so excited. There must be a million of those dogs around. You can't be sure it's Tex."

A woman walked out the front door and called the dog to her side. I watched as the big dog obeyed her command; she took him by the collar and led him into the house. Parker followed.

"Oh, yeah? Now I'm sure that's Tex."

"How do you know?" Jason quizzed.

"Because that was Olive who just took him inside."

Chapter Nineteen

We sat in the car watching the closed front door, waiting for someone to come out. "I don't get it. Clancy and Olive? They can't be involved in all this," I said.

"Why not? You said he found that boat back in November. He could have found the *Gigabyte* months ago," Jason postulated. That scenario hadn't occurred to me, but Jason's theory sent my brain on a wild detour. I processed it, but couldn't make any sense out of it.

"But why all the charade? It doesn't fit. There's something else going on," I insisted.

Jason adjusted the strap of his seatbelt. "What do you want to do? Bust in there like the Lone Ranger?"

"No. Let me see your phone again, Tonto."

I punched in the number for Dan Cooper's office again, and navigated my way back to his voice mail. This time, he'd added an addendum to his announcement. "If this pertains to an urgent matter, press zero and speak with my assistant, Marci Eisman. She will assist you."

I pressed zero and waited for the welcome voice of a real person. "Hi. Marci Eisman, please?"

"One moment."

Ten seconds later, "This is Marci. Can I help you?"

"Hi Marci. My name is Devonie Lace. I've been—"

"Miss Lace. Yes. I've been expecting your call. I have a message for you from Agent Cooper. He's on his way to San Diego right now. He wants you to meet him at the FBI office there as soon as you can."

I checked my watch. "It'll have to be tomorrow morning. Can you relay that to him?"

"Certainly."

A moment later, the door I'd been watching swung open, and Stan Parker rushed out, followed by Clancy and Olive. Tex squeezed through the door, and Olive grabbed his collar and ordered him back into the house.

"Thanks, Marci," I blurted into the phone and hung up.

Stan, Clancy, and Olive piled into the minivan and peeled out of the driveway.

I pointed toward the escaping vehicle. "Quick! Follow them!"

Jason fumbled with the keys.

"Come on! Come on!" I blurted.

"I'm trying! Lay off!" He finally got the Ford started and jammed it in gear. We took off after the minivan.

"Not so close," I ordered. "He'll make us."

Jason eased off the gas pedal. "Make us? You've been watching too many cop shows."

"Just don't lose him."

We wound our way back to the freeway and merged into the heavy traffic, headed north. Stan Parker must have shoved his foot to the floor, because the minivan surged ahead, almost rear-ending the car in front of him. He swerved around the obstacle.

"Speed up," I ordered.

Jason eased the Taurus around the Honda in front of us. The minivan weaved in and out of traffic, putting more distance between us.

"Hurry! He's getting away!" I hollered, bracing my hands on the dash. I felt a knot in my stomach as the tension built with each passing second.

Jason leered at me. "Just relax. I told you I want to live to see another day." He checked over his left shoulder and eased into the carpool lane. The minivan was well ahead of us. I glanced over at the speedometer. It read seventy-five.

"Come on, Jason. People are passing us!"

He gripped the wheel and pushed the accelerator down a little more. I watched the needle inch up to eighty.

"Okay, now you're keeping up with the commuters. How about catching that minivan," I barked, pointing through the windshield toward the vehicle that had almost disappeared from our view.

Jason's knuckles were white as we barreled down the freeway at eighty-five miles-per-hour, then ninety. I sat on the edge of my seat and strained to keep the minivan in sight.

"I think we're gaining on him," I said, as I took a deep breath to fight off the symptoms of hyperventilation. "Keep it up."

The minivan moved over to the third lane, then to the center lane.

I pointed at it. "He's moving over. We better stick with him."

Jason didn't make any move. I glanced over at him. "Come on, Jason. Change lanes."

Jason looked over his right shoulder. "I can't. There's no opening."

I checked over my shoulder. "Sure there is! Just make one! They won't hit you!"

Jason flicked on his turn signal. The car on our right bumper sped up.

"Jerk," I grumbled, as it held its position next to us.

The minivan changed lanes again. "He's gonna get off, Jason! Come on! Get over!"

"I can't! There's no open spot!"

The minivan made one last swerve and glided down the off-ramp. We barreled by at eighty-five miles-per-hour. "Great. We lost him," I moaned. I couldn't believe it. After all that effort—the flight, the daring phone call, flushing Stan Parker out—all for nothing. I absolutely hate wasted effort. I tried to come up with a way to save this failed mission.

Jason eased his foot off the accelerator. "Sorry, Dev. There was just no way."

I cranked around in my seat and tried to see where the minivan went. It was useless. He was long out of view. I turned back around and adjusted my seatbelt. I didn't say a word; I just stared out the windshield, gritting my teeth.

Jason glanced at me. "Come on, Dev. I'm sorry. There really was no way—"

I saw myself acting like a child before Jason got his sentence out. "I know. You're right. I'm just worried about Spencer." I checked my watch. "Our flight's not for another four hours. Let's head back to the Bates Building."

"What are you cooking up now?" Jason asked with a worried tone in his voice.

I pointed out the window toward a shopping mall, on the west side of the freeway. "There. Let's stop at Sears."

"Sears?"

"Yeah. Got your credit card handy?"

"Jeez! You're gonna break me!"

I led Jason through the tool section of the store. I gathered up a leather tool belt, a collection of screwdrivers, pliers, wire cutters, and strippers.

"What in the world are you up to?" Jason asked, standing in the middle of the aisle, feet apart and hands on hips.

I picked up a baseball cap, took his hand, and led him toward the counter. "You'll see."

Jason signed on the dotted line, and we marched out of Sears with our purchases.

"Okay. Time's ticking. Let's get over to the Bates Building," I instructed.

Jason glared at me. "Something tells me I'm not gonna like this."

"Relax, it'll be okay." Famous last words. I remember chanting those very words to my manager at San Tel, during those eleven days when the database had gone down, and I couldn't get it back up. I've tried hard to stay away from situations that call for those four little words. Apparently, I haven't tried hard enough.

We pulled into the Bates Corporation lot and parked behind a large garbage bin. It was late in the afternoon and the time limit imposed by our return flight to San Diego nagged at me. I pulled the price tags off the tools and placed them randomly in the belt. I stopped and looked at Jason. "This isn't gonna work."

He squinted at me. "What's not gonna work?"

"My plan. I need you to do something first."

"Something? What *something?*"

"It's easy. Just go into the lobby. There's a stack of newsletters on the table in the waiting area. Grab one and bring it back."

"Newsletter? Why?"

"You'll see. Hurry."

Jason shook his head, unbuckled his seatbelt, and climbed out of the Ford. He pointed his finger at me. "You'd better be right about this."

I watched him disappear through the glass entrance. A moment later, he reappeared with the rolled-up newsletter in his hand. He beamed a proud smile at me as he approached the car and slid into the driver's seat. "Here you go. Mission accomplished."

I snatched it up and flipped through the pages, stopping when I found what I was looking for. "Good. Now we have to find a copy machine."

"Copies?" Jason shot a grimace my way, then started the car.

"Yeah. Go to that shopping center we passed about two miles back. I saw a drugstore," I recalled.

We stood at the copy machine, next to the ice-cream counter in the drugstore. I patted my pockets and glanced at Jason. "Got any change?"

He dug through his pockets and produced two .

dimes, four nickels, and six pennies. I picked out everything but the pennies.

I opened the newsletter to the sample forms and found the new design for the Bates Corporation work order. I tore off a small strip of blank paper from a different page, licked it, and pasted it across the word "sample" on the work order. I laid it facedown on the glass, closed the lid, put my dime in, and pressed the big, green button. The machine spit out half of a work order, too small, and oriented the wrong way on the paper.

Jason elbowed me. "Better read the instructions, techno-queen. That's all the change I have."

I smirked at him, pressed some buttons, dropped another dime in the slot, and hit the "Go" button, again. This time, it was perfect. I made two more copies and snatched the newsletter from the glass.

I took Jason's arm. "Come on. Let's go."

"Wait a minute. I'm gonna get an ice cream."

"Come on! We don't have time!"

Jason mimicked me in a high-pitched, nasally voice. "Come on, Jason. Give me your credit card, Jason. Drive me here, Jason. Drive me there, Jason. Jump off that cliff, Jason."

While ignoring his mockery, I dragged him through the exit door. "Give me the keys," I demanded.

"No."

"Then quit whining."

We parked in the Bates Building lot again. I scribbled some words on the work order and signed Stan Parker's name to it. I climbed out of the Taurus and stood next to the passenger door. Jason watched as I buckled the tool belt and wiggled it on my hips, to make sure it wouldn't slip off. "Wait here," I said.

"What are you up to?" Jason interrogated.

"I'm gonna see what I can dig up. If I'm not out of there in . . ." I checked my watch. ". . . in thirty minutes, come get me."

"Get you? But—"

I slammed the door and trotted across the parking lot toward the entrance, leaving Jason with his mouth hanging open. I slipped on a pair of sunglasses and tucked my hair through the opening in the back of the baseball cap.

When I pushed through the big glass door, I was relieved to see a different receptionist behind the counter. I removed my sunglasses and spread the work order out on the counter in front of her. "Hi. I'm from maintenance. I need to tone out some lines in Stan Parker's office."

The receptionist glanced over the work order, then back at me. "Where's your employee badge?"

I glanced at my watch. "By this time, it's probably somewhere in my backyard. My dog ate it last night."

She crinkled her nose. "Ew."

"Human Resources knows. I'm supposed to pick up a visitor badge from you, until they get my new one made up."

She pressed some buttons on her switchboard and smiled at me. I tapped my foot on the tile floor and readied to dash out the front door.

She glanced at her clock. "No one answers in Human Resources." She handed me a visitor badge. "Here. Just bring it back when you get your replacement."

"Thanks." I clipped the badge to my shirt and hurried down the corridor.

I glanced down a row of cubicles and checked my watch. It was nearly five. Restless employees packed up their things and made small talk, while they watched the hand on the clock sweep past the twelve. I strolled down the aisle and watched as the obedient employees logged off of their computers before going home for the night.

I rounded the corner and smiled at the last group of worker bees to leave the office. I watched them disappear around the corner and continued to peek into all the work stations. My heart raced, when I spotted the blank monitor with a sheet of paper taped to the screen. It read, "DO NOT TOUCH!" I removed the paper and bumped the mouse to deactivate the screen-saver. An update was running on the machine and apparently would run overnight. I minimized the running job and opened up the explorer window. Bingo. This client was logged into the network. I searched through folders, looking for any documents relating to Aziz. I kept getting "permission denied" messages. The user logged onto this machine didn't have access to the directories I needed. I shoved the chair back and jumped out of the seat.

I wandered around the first floor, lost. I finally hunted down a janitor, who directed me to Stan Parker's office. Stan had left in such a hurry, he failed to lock his door. I slipped in and sat down in front of his computer, which he'd also failed to log off of. I must have really panicked him with my call. His screen-saver password glared at me, daring me to try it.

I glanced around the sterile-looking office. There

were not many clues about hobbies, interests, loved ones—in fact, the only hint that he had a life outside this office was a photo of him and a small boy of about eight or nine, fishing from a pier. The San Francisco skyline was etched in the background, and they were laughing and obviously enjoying each other's company. I assumed it was his son.

Stan Parker was not a savvy computer user, but I was hanging my hat on the chance that he, at least, had administrator privileges to the network. I tapped my fingernails on the desk and stared at the screen, still prompting me for a password. I checked my watch. I only had twenty minutes before Jason would come to my rescue.

I remembered something Spencer told me, back when we worked for San Tel. I slid the keyboard closer and typed the word "password" in the designated box. I hit the enter key, and the screen-saver disappeared. "Shame on you, Mr. Parker," I whispered as I opened the explorer window and scrolled through the folders. I found one labeled "aziz" and brought up the first of six documents contained in it. A local printer was connected to Parker's computer and sat on a table in the corner of his office. I clicked on the print button and let the document finish spooling to the printer, before I brought up the next document.

I checked my watch. I'd have to be on my way out in five minutes. "Hurry up," I whispered as I impatiently waited for the printer to spit out the last two documents. I snatched them up and raced out of the office.

I stepped into the lobby in time to see Jason standing outside the locked glass doors. I smiled at him and pushed my way through.

"How was I supposed to come get you, when the doors were locked?" he grumbled.

"Doesn't matter. Let's go."

As we headed for the airport, I read through the stack of paper I'd generated in Parker's office. "Oh, man! We hit paydirt!" I blurted, bolting upright in my seat. I skimmed rapidly through the pages in my lap.

Jason glanced at me. "What? What's it say?"

"You won't believe this. Remember all those rumblings about an antitrust lawsuit the government threatened Gerald Bates with last year?"

"Yeah. I think so. Haven't heard much about it lately."

"And you're not gonna, either. They cut some sort of deal with Bates."

"Deal?"

"Yeah. He had established rapport with Mohammed Aziz, you know, that oil guy I told you about," I explained, as I continued reading. "Looks like they got to be pretty friendly. Aziz bought a Mercedes and gave it to Bates as a gift." I stopped for a moment and re-read the sentence. "Huh, this is weird. Aziz bought the car in San Diego and had it delivered to Bates's home. I wonder why he'd buy it there when Bates lives in the Bay area?" I pondered the question for a moment, then dismissed it. "Anyhow, the government wanted Bates to help get undercover agents into Iraq. Looks like they were supposed to pose as Bates's employees: aids, assistants, secretaries."

"What happened to Bates?" Jason interrupted, keeping his eyes on the road.

"Don't know. Nothing here says. Dan Cooper's our best bet, right now."

We turned in the rental car and rode the shuttle bus to the airport terminal. Our flight was delayed thirty minutes. Jason nudged me. "I'm gonna get a hotdog. Want anything?"

I pondered my choices. "Yeah. See if they have some kind of chicken sandwich—not deep-fried."

"If they don't?"

"I don't care. Anything. I'm starving." I knew it was risky giving Jason free reign to choose my food, but I was desperately hungry.

He came back with two hotdogs, smothered in mustard, ketchup, and relish. I didn't say a word, as I practically inhaled the preservative-packed wiener. I hated to admit it, but it tasted wonderful. I just blocked out everything I ever heard about what goes into hotdogs.

We touched down in San Diego and pushed our way through the congestion at the gate.

We started down the corridor toward the exit, when Jason pointed toward the restroom sign. "I'll be right back." He disappeared through the door, and I leaned against the wall to wait for him.

I noticed two uniformed men talking with each other. They glanced at me, then conferred some more. I moved away from the wall and started for the ladies' room. They beat me to it. One on each side of me, they took my arms and ushered me down the hall.

I stumbled over my own feet. How could they have

found me? They were just waiting for me, like a pair of cats at the mouth of a mouse hole. I glanced up and noticed the odd panels placed strategically in the ceiling. Cameras. They must have caught me on video in the San Francisco airport. It would have been a piece of cake to track down my destination and lay in wait. How could I have been so stupid? "What are you doing?" I exploded.

"Devonie Lace?" the one on my right asked.

"What do you want? Let me go!" I struggled to free my arms.

"You're under arrest. You have the right to remain silent—"

"Under arrest! For what?" I demanded.

The man in blue released my right arm and pulled the arrest warrant from his pocket. He read down the list. "Let's see. Where to begin: Grand theft, auto; assault with a deadly weapon; forgery; possession of narcotics with the intent to sell; driving under the influence—"

I cut him off. "You forgot fishing without a license," I hissed.

The officer smoothed out the crumpled sheet of paper in his hand and ran his finger down the list. "Give me a minute. I'm sure I can find that in here somewhere."

"You've got to be kidding. This is some kind of setup. I didn't do any of those things," I insisted.

My captors smiled, and the one still grasping my arm winked at his partner. "Funny, that's what they all say."

"But it's true. You've got to believe me. I've been framed."

"Tell it to the judge," the one on my left replied, as he and his partner hauled me down the long corridor and continued informing me of my rights.

I wasn't interested in their version of the Miranda speech. I'd heard it a thousand times on old "Dragnet" reruns. I cranked my head around to see Jason wander out of the men's room. I called out to him. "Jason! Call Dan Cooper!"

Jason gawked at the two officers escorting me away. "Where are they taking you?" he hollered.

I turned to the usher on my right. "Where are we going?" I gritted through my teeth as I gave up my struggle.

"Eighth Precinct."

I called back over my shoulder: "Eighth Precinct! Hurry!"

Chapter Twenty

I slumped in the back of the black-and-white squad car as it worked its way through the heavy traffic of San Diego. I stared blankly at the metal grate separating me from officers Robins and Cowen. They [conversed] as though I didn't exist. As far as they were concerned, anything behind the grate was on equal ground with rattlesnakes and rabid skunks. As we passed the "Eighth Precinct" sign, Cowen swung the car into the parking lot. On the other side of a tall chain-link fence, I noticed an unusual car. It was a bright pink Mercedes Benz. Robins noticed it, too.

"Oh, no. Mrs. Grovesner's at it again," Robins grumbled.

Cowen chuckled under his breath. "You'd think with the kind of money her husband brings home she could kick the habit."

"You kidding? I bet she shoplifts on purpose to pay him back for giving her that ridiculous pink car," Robins shot back. They both laughed.

I noticed the license plate frame as we passed by the Mercedes. It was from Grovesner Mercedes, a dealership in downtown San Diego.

Cowen parked the squad car in a slot close to the police station. "He probably got it for next to nothing.

Couldn't sell the thing on his lot—not with a paint job like that."

Cowen set the brake, cut the engine, and broke into his tour guide routine. "Here we are. And on your left, we have the historic Eighth Precinct building, home of the next Pig Bowl champions of the Southland."

Robins pulled me from the back seat and slammed the door. He grinned at his partner. "Those CHP wimps are gonna cry to their mamas after Saturday's game."

I glared at the cavalier pair as they led me up the steps. As we entered the building, a well-dressed woman walked toward us, heading for the exit. She had mascara-stained tear streaks down both cheeks, and one of her teal-green pumps had a broken heel, causing her to limp like a pathetic, broken-down old horse. Her outfit was expensive, probably from one of the finer department stores in the area. Her perfume was strong, but not unpleasant. Its scent arrived well in advance of her physical self, and I thought she could probably stand to be a little more conservative when applying it. I noticed the huge diamond ring on her left hand. She wiped her nose with a wad of tissue and tried to avoid our stares.

Officer Cowen held the door open for her and gave a huge smile as she passed. "Evening, Mrs. Grovesner," he greeted.

She nodded and mumbled something I couldn't hear as she scurried out of the building. I would have shed a tear for the poor thing if I hadn't already been feeling so sorry for myself.

My delightful evening ended by being ushered into a cold, dreary, holding cell. The unconcealed, stainless steel commode in the corner sent a shiver up my spine.

I wondered how long I could hold out without using it and wished I hadn't drank that last glass of water on the plane.

I laid on the hard bunk for hours and stared up at the gray ceiling. The place wreaked of Pine Sol®, trying to cover up all the other unpleasant odors, but not succeeding. Women in neighboring cells shouted obscenities at each other, revealing their true natures, and making it perfectly clear to me why they were here in the first place. But why was I here? I felt the tears welling up. I knew I'd just about reached the end of my "tough-woman" performance, and the true Devonie, the scared little girl who desperately wanted someone to rescue her, was about to burst out into uncontrollable sobs. I squeezed my eyes shut and tried to redirect my focus.

"When do I get my phone call?!" I yelled at the top of my lungs, assuming no one was listening. I bolted upright when I heard the jingling of keys clanking against the lock on my cell. The voice on the other side laughed and said, "Just settle down, little Miss 'I've-been-framed.' " The bars swung open and a hefty woman in a drab uniform marched in. The guard pointed at me. "You got a ticket out of here, Missy. Got friends down at the FBI, do we?"

I raised my eyebrows and held my hand to my chest. "Me?"

"Yes, you, girl. Come on."

I followed the guard out of the cell and down the hall. We pushed through a door. My eyes lit up when I saw Jason and Dan Cooper waiting for me.

"Am I glad to see you guys. I was afraid I'd be

spending the night here." I let out a sigh of relief as Jason put a comforting arm around my shoulders.

Dan shook his head and wagged his finger at me. "What sort of trouble are you in now?"

Funny. Instead of feeling afraid, I felt embarrassed. For the second time in my recent past, I required the help of the FBI to get out of a life-threatening situation. For someone who's long-term goal was to attain a carefree, happy-go-lucky existence, I'd failed miserably. "Big trouble," I moaned.

"I guess so. Had to pull some mighty big strings to get you released to my custody. Officially, you're my prisoner."

"Well, get me out of here. You won't believe the story I have for you this time."

I sat in the passenger seat of Dan's car and listened to Jason point out every fast-food restaurant between the Eighth Precinct and the San Diego Marriott. Dan pulled into the hotel parking lot and drove around to the back.

"Got you a room on the seventh floor. Jason can crash in my room."

I eyed the elegant hotel's hedges, shimmering in the moonlight. It was almost eerie, without so much as a leaf moving. The grounds were immaculate—perfectly manicured. The palms were flawlessly trimmed. Lights shone on every tree. "Jeez. Tax dollars keep you up in style."

Dan pointed his finger at me. "Hey! Don't complain, or I'll put you up at the Motel 6 down the road."

I checked my watch: two in the morning. "You think room service is still operating? I'm starving."

Dan opened his door. "I doubt it. Room's got a snack bar. Help yourself. It's on the taxpayers." He winked.

We rode the elevator to the seventh floor and Dan let Jason into his room. Jason plopped down on one of the beds and was out cold before his head hit the pillow.

Mine was the adjoining room. Dan handed me the key and followed me in. I made a beeline for the bathroom, and he sat down in one of the chairs by the window. I washed my hands and splashed cool water on my face. Feeling somewhat refreshed, I wandered back out to the room and collapsed on the bed.

"Now, don't you fall asleep yet. I want the *Reader's Digest*, condensed version of this fiasco—right now. In the morning, you can fill in the details." Dan sat at the table and scribbled some notes in his little black notebook.

I laid on my back and stared at the ceiling. "Jeez. Where do I start? It's all a blur. Oh, yeah. It started back in Long Beach, when I bought the trunk from Clancy."

The last thing I remember mumbling was something about Mohammed Aziz, and how I wondered where he fit into the picture.

I was deep in one of my Tom Selleck dreams when the phone on the nightstand rang in my ear and startled me out of my happy little fantasy. I glared at the clock. Seven a.m. My hand reached for the phone and dragged it across the pillow to my head.

"Wake up, Sleeping Beauty," Dan Cooper's voice boomed cheerily into my ear.

"You've got a lot of nerve, waking me up at this hour," I grumbled into the phone.

"I've got places to go, people to see. Rise and shine. Come on. Breakfast here is great! I'll give you ten minutes."

"I don't know what planet you're from, but typical Earth women require a *minimum* of twenty minutes to get presentable in the morning—and that's just barely presentable. I'll need thirty, at least," I groaned. I clumsily hung up the phone and staggered out of bed. My number-one priority was to find a toothbrush and a long shower.

I sat in the corner booth between Jason and Dan. Jason ordered pigs-in-a-blanket. Dan watched, incredulously, as Jason proceeded to smear mustard and ketchup on his breakfast. He looked up at the two of us gawking at his plate. "What? It's not that much different than a hotdog," Jason defended.

Dan shook his head, raised his coffee cup to his lips, took a long sip, then set it down on the table. "I made some calls this morning. Your hunch was right about Mohammed Aziz. He is in town. Has a place here somewhere. Showed up a couple days ago with a friend."

I swallowed a bite of my bran muffin. "Friend?"

"Yeah. One of the bad guys. Known terrorist. We keep a close eye on our Middle-Eastern visitors. Haven't given us any clues what they're up to yet."

I shoved a whole strawberry in my mouth, bit it twice, and struggled to keep the juice from running down my chin, before I tried to speak. "Great. You must know where they are. We can go check them out," I announced, eager for his agreement.

He smirked at me. "There'll be no 'we.' "

"But I want to—"

"But, nothing. You've managed to get yourself in enough trouble."

"I can help, really—"

"When I need your help, I'll let you know. Until then, you do as I say. Got it?"

"No, I don't 'get it.' Spencer could be in real trouble and it's my fault. How can you expect me to just sit here and do nothing?" I persisted.

"Are you hearing impaired?" Dan complained.

Jason laughed. "That's funny. She is hardheaded, isn't she? I like to think of her as 'authority challenged.' "

I glared at them both. "Go ahead, mock me, but it's a free country, last I checked, and you can't keep me prisoner here against my will."

"Correction: You *are* my prisoner, remember? Willis and I can go check out Aziz and his amigo. He's meeting me here at ten. You, my dear, are planting your little fanny in that hotel room upstairs, and young Jason, there, is going to make sure you stay put." He pointed a threatening finger at me.

"Willis? But I—"

"Yes, Willis. You remember him? My partner? The one who's highly trained in dealing with terrorists. The one who can shoot the cap off a beer bottle at a hundred yards. The one I trust with my life."

I slid two inches down in the booth, like a child who'd just been scolded for talking in church. He'd taken the wind out of my sails by reminding me that I wasn't nearly as free as I thought.

Jason gulped down the last swallow of his Coke, then signaled the waitress for a refill. "Don't worry, Dan. I'll make sure she stays out of trouble. Some great movies are playing on Pay-Per-View. We'll just veg out in front of the TV until you get back."

I smirked at Jason, then turned to Dan. "That's right. We'll just become vegetables and sit idly in front of the idiot box, waiting for your return." The sarcasm in my voice was obvious.

"Good."

Dan paid the bill, then escorted Jason and me back up to his room. I filled Dan in on every detail I could think of since the whole caper started back in Long Beach. At 9:45, the phone in Dan's room rang. He grabbed it.

"Cooper. Oh, hey, Tom. I'll be down in five. Meet me in the lobby." Dan hung up the phone. "Okay. I'm out of here."

He stood and pointed his finger at me. "You, young lady, had better not budge from this room."

Jason grabbed the remote control off the nightstand. "Not to worry. I'm in charge now." He turned on the TV and started flipping through the channels.

Dan flashed me an uneasy smile, then let himself out of the room.

I parted the curtains and glanced down the seven floors to the parking lot. A collection of cabs were lined up along the curb, waiting to take busy travelers to the airport, or wherever else they needed to go. I watched Dan Cooper and Tom Willis pile into their government issue car and pull out into the heavy traffic. I thought about Spencer and what kind of trouble he might be in. The heavy weight of guilt felt like it might overwhelm me. A vision of Spencer flashed through my mind: Spiderman pajamas, red toenails, little red wagon, slurping up milk from the bottom of a bowl of Captain Crunch cereal. Just an innocent guy caught up in *my* crazy misfortune. I couldn't just sit there and do nothing.

"I'm gonna get some ice," I announced.

"Ice? What for?" Jason demanded.

"Because I want ice, okay?"

"I'll get it."

"Don't you trust me?"

"About as far as I can throw you. You're up to something."

"I'm getting ice. I'll be right back," I insisted.

I marched out of the room. The elevator was at the other end of the long hallway. I sprinted for it. Jason's voice followed me down the corridor. "Darn you, Devonie! Get back here! Let the authorities handle this!"

The elevator door closed with me inside right before Jason reached it. I smiled and waved to him. I pushed the button for the lobby and felt my stomach rise as the elevator descended. I contemplated how I was going to pay the cab fare, but decided I'd cross that bridge when I got to it.

The elevator doors opened and dropped a bomb on my proverbial bridge. Dan Cooper and Tom Willis stood in front of me, smiling. They each took one giant step into the elevator and grabbed my arms. Dan pressed the button for the seventh floor.

I gawked at them. "But . . . you left . . . I saw your car—"

Dan slung his heavy arm over my shoulder. "Figured you were watching. We just made a quick trip around the block. A little test, I guess you'd say." Dan looked over at his partner, Tom Willis. "I'd say she failed, wouldn't you, Tom?"

Tom nodded his head. "Big time."

"Now. You're not gonna try it again, right?" Dan lectured.

I nodded.

"And where are we going right now?" he continued.

"Room seven twenty-eight?" I replied as innocently as I could.

"That's right. Do I need to put an armed guard at the door?"

"No. I'll be good. I promise."

"Good."

The elevator doors opened to reveal Jason, ready to jump in. Dan marched me out of the elevator. "You let me down, Jason," Dan said.

"I know. Sorry. She's just so . . . so . . ."

"Hardheaded?" Dan offered.

"That, too."

I plopped down on the bed and watched the opening credits roll for some action-packed thriller, guaranteed to keep me on the edge of my seat to the very end.

Jason scowled at me. "Don't you try that again. I promised Dan I'd keep you out of trouble."

I scowled back at him. "Be quiet. I'm trying to watch the movie."

Chapter Twenty-One

Jason ordered us room service for lunch. I had no change to tip the bellboy. I gave Jason the same look my mother used to give my father when he failed to compliment Grandma on her cooking. Jason was clueless. Finally, I stuck my elbow in his ribs. "Are you going to tip him or should I offer to wash his car?"

"Huh? Oh, right." Jason handed him a dollar and then lifted the lid off his entree.

I sat Indian style on the bed, with my lunch tray spread out in front of me. I took a bite of a carrot, then picked up the phone. I dialed my number and listened to my messages as my crunching echoed in my ear. My jaw quit grinding the food, much the same way a horse stops chewing when startled by a sudden sound. I perked up my ears and listened.

Jason noticed my sudden concern. He sat on the edge of the chair and watched me. "What? What?"

I shushed him and held the phone tighter, my free hand covering my other ear to muffle outside noise.

I replayed the message. His voice was barely audible. "Devonie. It's Spencer. Call your friend at the FBI. That Aziz guy—he's one of 'em. If we don't stop 'em by three, it's all over for—oh, jeez, they're coming. I'm at . . . shoot . . . where the heck am I? Man,

I've gotta get out here. I'll call you back in—" Click. The line went dead.

I pushed my lunch tray out of the way and scrambled for my shoes. "Come on. We've gotta get going."

"No way. Dan said to stay—"

"I know what Dan said. Spencer's in trouble. Real trouble. If we don't get to him by three—I don't even want to think about what might happen. You coming or not?"

"Where?"

"I'm not sure yet." I flipped open the *Yellow Pages*. My finger ran down the list of car dealers in San Diego, until it landed on the one I was after. "Let's go."

Jason complained nonstop as he withdrew eighty dollars from the ATM machine in the hotel lobby. "Dan's gonna kill me for letting you do this," he grumbled.

I flagged down a cab, and we jumped in the back. "Harbor and Twenty-ninth," I blurted.

The cab driver took the toothpick out of his mouth and dropped it in the ashtray. "Sure thing. You two on vacation?"

Jason started to chat. "Oh, no. We both live—"

"Yes. We're on vacation. From Ohio. San Diego's such a beautiful city." I flashed my mother's look at Jason again.

"Right. Ohio. Brought the little woman out West to see some stars." Jason winked at me. I rolled my eyes.

The cabby smiled at us in the rear-view mirror. "Ohio. My sister's in Ohio. What part you from?"

I racked my brain for a city name. "The middle."

Jason shot me a sideways glance and mouthed the word "middle?" at me.

The cabby chuckled. "What city, I mean?"

"Oh. Uh . . . Toledo," I stammered.

Jason shook his head at me.

"Toledo? Isn't that up north?" The cabby glanced over his shoulder to change lanes.

I searched Jason's expression. He nodded at me. "Yes, it is. When I said middle, I meant the middle-of-nowhere."

The cabby laughed. I changed the subject as quickly as I could.

Jason paid the fare. We were barely three steps out of the cab, when we were greeted by a salesman at the sidewalk. "Good afternoon. Welcome to Grovesner Mercedes. Can I show you one of the most beautiful cars in the world?"

I flashed him a smile. "Actually, I'm here to see Mr. Grovesner. Is he in?"

"Lou? Yeah, I think so. Right inside." He pointed out a man to us through the glass windows. "That's him, there."

"Thanks," I said.

Jason followed me inside. I approached the man identified as Lou. He was busy reading through a contract. "Excuse me. Mr. Grovesner?"

He looked up from his papers. "Depends. You from the IRS?"

I exchanged a glance with Jason.

"Just kidding. I'm Lou Grovesner. What can I do for you?" He held his hand out for me to shake, then to Jason.

"I need your help, Mr. Grovesner."

"Please . . . Lou. What is it? I aim to please."

"I need the address of someone who bought a car from you recently."

"Address? I'm sorry, but I can't give out that kind of information. Privacy laws, you know."

I wonder when it was that we voted on all these laws. There's a law for everything these days. "It's really important. Someone's life may depend on it."

"I'm sorry. I didn't catch your names," Lou continued.

"Devonie Lace. This is—"

"Jason. Jason Walters," Jason offered.

"Devonie. I'd like to help you out, but I just can't bend the rules."

Couldn't this man take what I said at face value and have enough heart to help, regardless of the rules? I glanced around the showroom. There were a dozen people milling around, admiring the luxury cars. "Do you have an office where we can talk privately?"

"I do, but we can talk here, Devonie. There's just no way—"

"I saw your wife yesterday, Lou," I interrupted, looking as concerned as I could.

Lou raised a brow. "My wife? But she was . . . yesterday?"

"That's right. Eighth Precinct. She seemed like a very compassionate person. Maybe she could convince you to help me."

Lou took me by the arm. "My office is this way."

Lou escorted us into his private office. Jason and I sat across from him at his desk. "Now what kind of scam are you trying to pull?" His pleasant, aim-to-please voice turned sour.

"It's no scam, Lou. A friend of mine is in terrible danger, and Mohammed Aziz is the cause of it. I need to find him. You sold him a car recently; you must have an address where he's staying in San Diego."

Lou fiddled with a mechanical pencil, dropping the long, thin lead on the floor. "You saw my wife?" he asked, as he bent over to pick up the lead.

"Yes. Lovely woman, but very sad. You should try to get her some help." I scooted to the edge of my seat. "Please, Mr. Grovesner. You'd be doing a good thing by helping me; otherwise, I might have to go to my friend down at the *Tribune*. He sometimes can get information for me, but he usually wants something in return."

Lou put the pencil back in its holder. His lips straightened into a tight, thin line. "That won't be necessary. I'll be right back." Lou rolled his chair out from behind the desk and stalked out of the room.

Jason waited for the door to close. "What've you got on him?"

"His wife is . . . well . . . I'll tell you later."

"What? Tell me now. How do you know his wife?"

"She was in jail yesterday."

Jason's eyes lit up. He wanted the dirt and he wanted it now.

Lou popped his head back in. "Just one more minute. I'm having one of the girls get that address for you."

I smiled at him. "Thanks, Lou."

Five minutes later, Lou returned with a yellow sticky note. An address and phone number were scribbled on it. He handed it to me. "You didn't get this from me, or anyone else here. Deal?"

I nodded and slipped the paper in my pocket. Lou walked to the door and waited for us to leave, with not so much as a polite smile.

I stood up and Jason followed my lead. "Thank you, Lou. I really appreciate this." I checked my watch. "You know, you should take your wife out to lunch—maybe even a matinee. She's probably just crying out for some—"

"Thanks for the advice." His eyes shot up toward the ceiling. "I'll think about it. Now, if you'll excuse me, I've got work to do."

The taxi dropped us off in front of Jason's house. I slid out of the cab and waited, while Jason paid the fare. I watched as Jason's neighbor wandered slowly around the Jeep parked in his driveway, periodically bending over to peer under the vehicle. When he saw Jason arrive home, he strolled over to the curb.

"Hey, Jason."

Jason turned to greet him. "Matt! You're back. How was the vacation?"

"Great! Not long enough."

I smiled and nodded with total understanding.

"Something weird, though. You see anyone messing with my Jeep? Plates are gone," Matt informed us.

I held my breath for a moment. I'd managed to really make Jason mad at me over the last couple days. He could get even right about now.

"Really? No, man. I didn't see anything," Jason lied.

"Huh. Guess I'll have to make a trip to the DMV—get a new set."

Jason shook his head in sympathy. "Bummer."

"Yeah. Well, thanks for feeding Barney."

"Any time. Catch ya later."

The puzzled man wandered back to his Jeep and checked underneath it again. He shook his head and drifted back toward his house, glancing one more time at the plateless vehicle parked in his driveway.

Jason disappeared into the house, long enough to retrieve his keys. I waited in the driveway by his truck.

I jumped into the passenger seat, and he slid in behind the wheel. "Okay, where to?" he asked with more eagerness than I expected.

I pulled the address from my pocket. "Coronado."

I've heard it referred to as an island, but technically, it's not. Coronado is connected to California by a long, narrow strip of land from the south, known as the Silver Strand. Silver Strand Boulevard is one of only two roadways that provide access to Coronado. The other is a bridge linking the "almost island" to Harbor Drive.

Jason merged with the heavy traffic to cross the bridge. I paged through his *Thomas Guide* until I found the street name printed on my little yellow sticky note. I directed Jason to the house.

House is not the appropriate word to describe the structure. Mansion would do it more justice. Brick of various shades of red, charcoal, and ash-white formed pillars that stood about fifteen feet apart and surrounded the grounds. Black wrought iron formed the fence that protected the estate from the common folks. The perfectly-manicured lawn hadn't a weed in sight. Pink and white begonias lined the horseshoe-shaped driveway that led to the manor. The house was made of the same brick that formed the fence pillars. Arches at the entryway boasted huge hanging pots of fuchsia, and fiery bougainvillea vines crept along the walls around the windows.

Jason pulled to the curb. I checked my watch; 2:20. "Don't park here. That's Dan's car." I pointed at the dark-blue sedan parked across the street with the two FBI agents sitting inside.

Jason glanced at the car. "So let's go tell him about the message from Spencer. That's why we're here, isn't it?"

"I will. You know he'll be mad as heck to see us here. I want to check things out first. Park over there," I said, pointing ahead through the windshield.

Jason put the truck in gear and pulled out to the street. We drove around the corner and parked behind what looked like the caretaker's quarters.

I swiveled around in the seat and peered at the closed iron gates. "Think there's another way in?"

Jason pressed the automatic door locks. "We don't want to go in there. The FBI has enough firepower here to handle things. They don't need Wonder Woman and her sidekick getting caught in the crossfire."

I unbuckled my seatbelt. "So, what, we're just gonna sit here and watch the show?" I grumbled. He knew me better than to expect any such thing.

"No. We're gonna deliver the message to Dan—if he doesn't kill us first for leaving the hotel."

Before I could get the rebuttal out of my mouth, a tall, lanky figure dashed out from behind a box-hedge next to the gardener's shack and raced across the lawn. I cranked my head around. "That's Spencer!" I unlocked the door and started to jump out of the truck.

Jason reached across the bench seat and grabbed my

belt loop. "Oh, no you don't. Look." He pointed toward the eight-foot-tall iron gate. A black Mercedes pulled to the entrance and waited for the automatic gate to swing open. We watched as the sleek car passed the barrier, the gate closing behind it.

Spencer disappeared behind the main house. I climbed back in the truck and kneeled backwards in the seat to watch Dan Cooper. He and Willis weren't moving. "They're just sitting there. Aren't they going to do something? Anything?" My heart was pounding in my chest.

"What should they do?" Jason asked.

"I don't know. Spencer's in there; they must know that. They should go in." A trillion thoughts raced through my head—none boding well for Spencer.

Jason bumped my shoulder. "Look." He pointed at the Mercedes. Two men got out of the car. One ran inside the house; the other loitered at the car, lit a cigar, and checked his watch.

I checked out Dan's car again. There was no action. "What the heck are they waiting for? A formal invitation?" As the seconds passed, my frustration escalated until my blood was ready to boil.

I watched, helplessly, as the man with the cigar wandered along the walkway toward the back of the house—toward Spencer. A moment later, he reappeared, tossed his cigar on the ground, and dashed to the front door. He banged on it, until someone let him in. That was all I could stand. "That's it. I've gotta go light a fire under Dan. He can punish me all he wants. Spencer's in trouble."

Jason grabbed my arm. "Are you gonna tell him I brought you here?"

"No. I'll tell him I flew, you big chicken."

Jason frowned. "Dan'll kill me when he finds out I drove you here. This was a terrible idea."

"Dan won't kill either of us, but someone may kill Spencer if you don't let go of me," I snapped. I yanked my arm away from Jason.

I slipped out of the truck and started for Dan's car. Before I could take three steps, the government issue sedan pulled away from the curb and sped off. "What the heck?" I watched as Dan and Tom disappeared around the corner. I shrugged my shoulders and exchanged a glance with Jason, who was equally as puzzled. "What now?" I wondered, studying my surroundings.

I gazed down the length of the iron fence, then up at the sharp points, about eight feet high. I turned on my heels, blasted past the hood of the truck, and sprinted toward the back side of the caretaker's house. A pruning ladder was propped against a huge oak tree, just outside the fence. I heard Jason cursing me, as I leaned it against the wrought iron and climbed over.

Once inside the grounds, I darted from hedge to bush, until I reached the house. I followed the path I thought I saw Spencer take around the back. I crept among the ornamental plants growing in the flowerbeds close to the building.

An unusual, but strangely familiar sound caught my attention. Click, click, click on the cement. I turned to see where it came from. *Uh oh. Dogs. Rottweilers. Two of them.* I spotted a lattice attached to the framework of a second-story deck, and my instincts told me to climb. I was halfway up before they reached me, snarling and spitting slobber with each bark. I struggled to pull myself over the railing to the deck.

The sliding glass door to the bedroom was halfway open. I slipped through the opening and peered at the lavish surroundings. The decor was early jungle: A four-poster bed sat in one corner, surrounded by a curtain of sheer mosquito netting; a live palm and two rubber-tree plants stood in the corner; a Casablanca-style ceiling fan turned slowly in the center of the room; framed posters of zebras, giraffes, elephants, and various big cats decorated the walls; a genuine leopard-skin rug was hanging in the opposite corner.

I tiptoed across the room toward the closed door. I turned the knob and peeked into the hallway. It was empty; so I slipped out of the room. I passed a half-dozen closed doors as I snuck down the long corridor. I placed my ear against each one to listen for Spencer.

I froze, like a deer-in-headlights, when the sound of footsteps came barreling up the stairs. My heart skipped a beat. I was paralyzed for a moment, then turned and reached for the nearest doorknob. I let myself into the room and quietly shut the door. Keeping my hand on the knob, I rested my forehead against the panel of the door and breathed deeply. I tried to slow the pace my heart. The footsteps pounded down the hall, then stopped. So did my breathing.

I didn't hear him come up behind me, but I felt his breath on my neck just before his hand reached around my face and covered my mouth. His other arm wrapped around my waist and pulled me away from the door. He dragged me backwards through the room, into the master bath. I struggled to get free, until I spotted the sight of the two of us in the full-length mirror. Spencer stood behind me, his reflection smiling like the Cheshire cat. He released his grip on me.

I started to speak, but he put his finger to his lips to shush me.

"What are you doing here?" I whispered.

He took me by the hand and led me out of the bathroom.

"Come on. We don't have much time," he whispered back.

I followed Spencer to the door. He opened it just a crack, and peeked through. We heard the muffled voices of two men downstairs. One shouted in a language I couldn't understand, but from the tone of his voice, it was clear he was barking orders.

We slipped through the door and eased our way along the wall toward the staircase. Spencer signaled for me to stay put, while he checked to see that the coast was clear. He got down on his hands and knees and crawled to the opposite end of the hall. He stood up and motioned for me to join him. I dropped to my knees and began crawling. When I reached the staircase, a voice at the bottom of the steps boomed. I couldn't understand the words, but when I saw nothing but hair, teeth, and eyeballs bounding up the stairs toward me, I didn't need a translator.

I got to my feet and leaped for Spencer. He opened the door he stood in front of; we dove inside and slammed it shut. I turned the lock on the solid-oak door and collapsed against it. A loud thud from the other side made me jump away. We stared at the solid panel door as our pursuer repeatedly crashed against it. "thank God for oak," I whispered.

Two more failed attempts to bust down the door,

and he gave up. Spencer and I glanced around our surroundings. We were in another bedroom. This one also had a balcony. I ran to the French doors and shoved them open. "Come on," I called.

Spencer and I stood on the deck and looked out over the rail. We had a full view of the front of the house and the street. Jason's pickup cruised slowly up the driveway, toward the closed gates.

Suddenly, the front doors burst open below us, and the two men ran out, dragging a third man, obviously against his will. I recognized Mohammed Aziz from his photo in the *Bates Corporation Newsletter.* The other captor was unfamiliar to me, and the struggling man never turned his face our direction.

Shaking his fist, Spencer leaned over the rail and yelled at the men. "Stop! Let him go!"

I strained to recognize the man. "Who is it?"

Spencer was halfway to the bedroom door before I got the sentence out. The abductors grappled with their captive, but soon overpowered him and threw him into the back of the Mercedes.

I started back into the bedroom to follow Spencer, when a loud bang caught my attention. Jason's truck crashed through the front gates as the Mercedes squealed away from the house. Jason swerved to miss it and accelerated through the flowers onto the lawn.

"Go, go, go!" I ran down the stairs on Spencer's heels. We blasted out the front doors. Jason stuck his foot to the accelerator, spinning his big tires in the grass. Clumps of sod and dirt flew as Jason left a pair of bare-earth tracks in the once-perfect turf. His truck skidded to a stop in front of us. The Mercedes was halfway down the street, almost out of sight.

Spencer and I piled into the pickup. "Follow him!" Spencer ordered. Jason jammed the truck into gear and shoved his foot to the floor.

I fumbled with the seatbelt as the truck swayed around the corner of the driveway. Spencer helped me get it buckled, then snapped his own around his waist.

The Mercedes disappeared around a corner, and Jason sped up to catch it. "Looks like he's headed for Silver Strand. Probably doesn't want to get caught in the bridge traffic," Jason said.

"Where the heck is Dan?" I raged.

Spencer put one hand on the dash and pointed through the windshield with his other. "They're turning, see?"

"I see," Jason confirmed as he pressed a little harder on the gas pedal.

I caught a glimpse of a street sign. "This is Silver Strand. If we don't catch him here, we're gonna lose him."

Jason shot me a glance. "I know. I'll do my best."

Spencer raised his pointing finger again. "Look! What's that?"

Flashing red and blue lights formed a solid line across the boulevard about a half mile in front of us. The Mercedes swerved in and out of traffic. Jason did the same. We managed to get within ten car lengths of it, before it slammed on its brakes. There were at least twenty police cars blocking the road at Silver Strand State Beach. There'd be no way for the Mercedes to get through.

Instead, it spun around and aimed straight for us. Jason put his foot on the brakes and slid the truck sideways, blocking most of the roadway. The Mercedes took to the beach. Jason hit the gas and paralleled the German car from the paved road. When we got in front of it, we swerved over, forcing it toward the water. Jason kept the pressure on, until the axles were submerged in saltwater. I couldn't believe Jason's daring moves. He was like a stunt driver in an action movie. Flashing lights and sirens headed our direction. By the time they reached us, the Mercedes was nearly floating in the surf. The case was over.

Dan Cooper's car skidded to a halt on the pavement. He and Tom Willis jumped out and ran toward the Mercedes with their guns drawn. I gawked, as I watched Stan Parker emerge from the back of Dan's car and race after them. Officers pulled Aziz and his counterpart out of the front seat of the Mercedes and dragged them through the surf to the beach. I gaped when I saw the man in the back seat escape from the floating vehicle. It was Gerald Bates.

Chapter Twenty-Two

I stood on the beach and watched a tow truck haul the Mercedes out of the surf. Aziz and his terrorist counterpart were loaded into the back of a police car and taken away. Dan Cooper strolled up behind me. "Back to the pokey for you, young lady."

I spun around. "But—"

"Just kidding. I ought to lock you up, though, for your blatant disregard for my authority." He winked at me. "You hungry? I'm buying."

I smiled. "You mean the taxpayers, don't you?"

"No. This time, it's on me. Really. Your friends, too."

I tried to remember my last meal. Oh yes, the hot-dog. I was starving. "Sounds great. I'll tell Jason and Spencer."

In the distance, Stan Parker stood next to Dan's car and glared at me. I replayed the threats I'd made to him over the phone in my mind. If looks could kill, I'd be cold and stiff.

Dan noticed the daggers in Stan's eyes. "By the way, what'd you do to Stan? To hear him tell it, you're about six years overdue for an exorcism."

"Did he tell you about it?"

"Won't say a word. I tried to invite him to dinner

with us. When I told him I'd be inviting you, he suddenly had to wash his hairpiece or something. What's the deal?"

I flashed my most charming smile across the beach at Stan Parker. He scowled and turned away. "I didn't know he was one of the good guys. I guess I pushed some wrong buttons when I flushed him out." I bit my lip and stared out over the Pacific. That awful feeling of guilt weighed on my shoulders again.

I touched Dan on the arm. "Give me a minute," I said, then meandered, unthreateningly, toward Stan Parker. He started to walk away at the sight of my approach.

"Hold up, Stan," I called to him.

"What do you want?" he asked, crossing his arms across his chest and planting his feet squarely in front of me.

"Peace offering. Please hear me out," I pleaded.

He stared at me, but didn't say a word.

"I'm really sorry about that phone call, but I thought you were a bad guy. My friend was missing, and I didn't know who to trust. You can understand that, can't you?" I explained.

He nodded, but still didn't speak. I could see this would be a hard sell.

"I knew you weren't what you claimed to be, so I assumed you were on the wrong side," I continued.

"You weren't what you claimed to be, either. That put you on the wrong side, too?" he countered.

I hadn't even considered that. Deception works on many levels, for many causes. "You're right, but can't we call a truce? Shake hands and make up?"

He dropped his hands to his sides. "Water under the bridge, so to speak?"

"Exactly. You know, I live on a sailboat. You have a son who likes to fish, don't you?" I baited.

His eyes lit up at the mention of his son. "Yeah. How'd you know?"

I didn't dare tell him about my spy mission in his office. "I think Dan mentioned it," I lied. Another instance of deception working in my favor. "I'd love to take you and your family out for a day on the water. Your son would have a blast."

I detected a hint of a smile in Stan's face. I think I was getting through that tough exterior. "I know he'd love it. I work a lot. We don't get to spend much time together."

I put my hands on my hips. "Well, that's it, then. You name the day, and we'll raise the sails and head for wherever the wind takes us. We'll pack a lunch and the poles and make a day of it. What do you say?" I dangled my offer out in front of him and hoped he'd snatch it up.

"You got a deal."

I beamed. "Great! Why don't you come with us to dinner, and we can work out the details."

Stan smiled and walked with me back across the beach, toward Dan and Tom. "Dan tried to tell me you were okay, even though. . . ."

"Even though what?" I asked.

"Nothing. He didn't say anything."

Dan Cooper, Tom Willis, Gerald Bates, Stan Parker, Spencer, Jason, and I sat around a big, private table at JoDee's Steak House. My eyes scanned down the menu at the list of entrees. "Don't they have salads here?"

Jason peered over his menu at me. "Salads are for sissies. Now, steak—that's a real man's meal."

Tom Willis took a swig from his mug of beer. "You got that right. Nothing like a big ol' slab of red meat to get the heart pumpin'."

The men seated around me echoed his sentiments. I smirked at them. "You mean, get your heart plugged up, don't you?"

Dan slapped his menu down on the table. "Let's change the subject, why don't we?"

I closed my menu and laid it on the table. "Good idea. What I want to know is: how did you know where to find Mr. Bates, Spencer?"

Spencer peeked out from behind his menu. "Who? Me?"

"Yes, you. When I got your message on my answering machine, I thought you were the one in trouble, but it was Bates they were planning to kill. How'd you know he was being held in Coronado?" I interrogated.

"That backup tape I stol—borrowed from Bates Corporation contained Stan's e-mail. I'd already figured out that the NSA forced Mr. Bates to help them get agents into Iraq to spy. They found out the Iraqis were producing billions of doses of toxins," Spencer explained.

"Toxins?" I repeated; my attention solidly on Spencer's words.

Gerald Bates offered a more detailed description. "Yes. The agents found a lab where they were producing botulinum toxin and ricin. Botulinum toxin is the most poisonous substance known to man. The whole body, including the respiratory system, becomes paralyzed, which leads to death by suffocation in just days."

I shuddered.

"And ricin . . . well you . . . heard about the umbrella murder in London, back in seventy-eight?" Bates continued.

I shook my head.

"A Bulgarian defector was jabbed in the leg with an umbrella. A tiny pellet containing a minute amount of ricin was implanted just under the skin. He was dead within a day," Bates said.

"That's incredible. But what does it have to do with Spencer?" I asked.

Spencer jumped back in. "I was getting to that. See, Mr. Bates e-mailed Stan that the agents discovered the lab and planned to take all the toxins and send them back to The States on his private jet. Stan is really the head of security for Bates Corporation, not the network administrator."

"We sort of guessed that, didn't we?" I grinned at Stan Parker, who sat across from me at the table. "Better not try to pass yourself off as a techno-geek, especially to the king of geeks."

Stan smiled, mildly embarrassed.

Spencer finished chewing a mouth full of sourdough bread and continued his story. "Anyhow, the e-mail said that Mr. Bates felt uneasy about the whole thing. He thought Aziz might be suspicious of him."

Bates spoke up. "That's putting it mildly. When the Iraqis discovered their chemical weapons had been stolen, they locked me up in my hotel room and put armed guards at the door. My jet got out of Iraq, but without me."

Stan proudly redeemed himself as a heroic figure. "So I gathered up a recovery team, trained them for six months; then we flew our little fannies into Iraq. Pulled off the sweetest rescue mission you've ever seen."

Bates smiled with appreciation at Stan and nodded. "In the meantime, the NSA off-loaded the toxins onto my yacht and sunk it to keep it out of the hands of the terrorists—and anyone else who might get crazy ideas about how to use it. The guy in charge of that operation was Morrison. Kent Morrison. He was supposed to record the location of the ship, so the toxins could be recovered at a later time. Anyway, the NSA came up with the story that I drowned to cover any connection they might have with me. They had no idea I was still alive."

I exchanged a glance with Spencer. "Morrison? We found his prints on the scuba tank."

"I know. No one's seen him since the *Gigabyte* went down. That's why the NSA lost track of the boat. They panicked. Billions of doses of lethal chemical weapons were sitting on the ocean floor not far off the coast of California, and no one knew where it was."

I shuddered at the thought. "And then I came along and found it. And Clancy! What about Clancy and Olive?" I pointed an accusing finger at Stan Parker. "You had Clancy and Olive!"

Stan held his hands up in self defense. "Clancy was determined to salvage that wreck. The NSA was prepared to make him disappear, if he didn't stay away. They'd threatened him and a friend of his."

"That would be Morgan Johnson. He was with me when I found the *Gigabyte*," I interjected.

Stan pointed his finger at me. "Right. Morgan co-operated with the NSA, but Clancy—he's the most hardheaded man I've ever met. Anyhow, I found out about the plans for Clancy and decided to hide him and his wife until this whole thing got resolved."

I chuckled. "Yeah, Clancy is a cantankerous old coot. But you've gotta like him. There's just something about him." I squeezed a fresh lemon slice into my water. "What about this Carissa West and her father, Harlan? How do they tie in?"

Dan decided to join in on the conversation. "Harlan West was Kent Morrison's partner—two peas in a pod. Both would stop at nothing to achieve an end, no matter what the means. He used his daughter's position with the Justice Department to hunt you down. They invented all those phony charges against you so they could haul you in. They knew you had information about the *Gigabyte* and they wanted it."

"What's going to happen to him?" I asked, as I picked the steamed broccoli off of Jason's plate.

"What do you mean?" Dan asked, slicing his steak.

"Like, is he going to jail?" I inquired.

"For what? His tactics may be a bit unsavory, but the rules most of us live by don't apply to everyone," Dan replied, then dipped his steak in a puddle of horseradish sauce and bit it off his fork.

"That's comforting. That still doesn't explain how Spencer found Mr. Bates," I replied, still a bit confused.

"If you'll just let me talk, I'll tell you," Spencer piped up.

"Go ahead, then," I prompted.

Spencer smiled. "Thank you. I read Stan's e-mails from the backup tape and figured out that Mr. Bates was still alive. I was finally able to hack into the Bates system and retrieved some encrypted files about the rescue mission. I found out—"

Gerald Bates pointed his finger at Spencer. "I've been meaning to speak to you about that. You hacked into my system? I've got the best firewall around, and you hacked it? I want to know how."

Spencer slipped three inches in his chair. "Well, it was for a good cause. I swear, I wouldn't have done it, if it weren't for—"

Bates put his hands up to stop Spencer's self-defense speech. "You want a job with Bates Corporation? Vice President of Information Technologies?" Bates offered.

"You're kidding, right?" Spencer coughed.

"Absolutely not. I'd rather have someone with your genius working for me, instead of against me," Bates continued.

"Funny. That's what the State of California said when they caught me hacking into their network," Spencer confessed.

"I imagine I can put you in a slightly better tax bracket than the State can. What kind of car do you drive?"

Bates asked.

"Dodge Dart. Almost a classic," Spencer boasted.

"How does a company car sound?" Bates dangled the proverbial carrot.

Spencer scratched his head. "Pantera?"

"Whatever floats your boat," Bates replied.

A huge smile spread on Spencer's face. "Cool."

I munched on a slice of cucumber from my salad. "Are you gonna finish telling me your story, Mr. Vice President?"

Spencer placed his fork on his plate. "Okay. So, there I am, at the United Express shack in San Francisco, waiting to get on the shuttle bus to take me to the main terminal, the day I was supposed to meet you."

"Yeah, and you never showed up," I reminded him.

"I know. I had a good reason. I'm standing on the tarmac, and I see a Bates Corporation jet land. Now, being the curious soul that I am, I watch, and who should get out of the plane but Gerald Bates, himself," Spencer said.

"That's incredible. I bet you were giddy," I said, picturing a star-struck Spencer, chasing after his hero.

Spencer nodded his head. "I was. Anyhow, he got into one of those little airport golf carts and drove off. I decided to see if I could follow him."

"You're kidding. You chased after him?" I asked.

Spencer shook his head. "No. I figured he'd either go to his office or home. I went back to my car and drove to his office. I knew where that was. When I got there, these two Arab-looking guys were hanging around the parking lot. One of them was puffing on a cigar. I recognized the other one as Mohammed Aziz, from that newsletter you picked up. When Mr. Bates showed up in his car, these two guys grabbed him and took off. I tried to follow them in my car, but it overheated going over the Altamont."

"So, how'd you find him?" I asked.

"Easy. I started hacking into county records and

found out Mohammed Aziz owns only one piece of property in California: the house in Coronado. I caught a flight to San Diego and checked it out myself. I ought to be a detective, don't you think?" Spencer boasted.

"I think you'll have enough fun being the newest Pantera-driving employee of Bates Corporation." I was suddenly reminded about my vehicle predicament. I caught Dan's attention. "Oh, by the way, my Jeep was stolen. I couldn't report it, because the entire police force was after me."

Dan peered at me over his glasses. "You need a ride somewhere?"

"I need my Jeep back. That's what I need," I informed him.

"And what do you want me to do about it?" Dan asked.

I rolled my eyes. "Well, shoot. You're the FBI, aren't you? Doesn't the 'I' stand for investigation?"

"Yeah, but not for old Jeeps," Dan answered.

"Old! That Jeep was clean as the day it rolled off the showroom floor," I argued.

Dan patted me on the head, like a little girl who has lost her doll. "Give it up, Dev. You just better hope you had insurance. Chances are you'll never see it again."

"Great." I started thinking about all the things I might not ever see again, besides my Jeep. I couldn't remember the last time I'd laid eyes on the *Plan C,* but I didn't really care. It was just a thing. All my stuff was just things. I shoved my chair out from the table. "I need to make a call. Anyone have change for the phone?"

Tom Willis dug some quarters out of his pocket. "Here you go."

"Thanks. Be right back."

I dialed the number and counted the rings. "Please be there," I whispered to myself. He answered on the fourth ring.

"Hey. It's me."

"Dev! Where are you? I went by your boat. I went by your Uncle's place. I've called a dozen times!"

I could hear the concern in Craig's voice. I felt terrible for neglecting the man who means more to me than anything else in the world. "I know. I'm sorry. It's a really long story, and I want to tell it to you."

"Are you okay? Where are you? I was ready to call out the National Guard to find you."

"I'm in San Diego having dinner with some friends. I was thinking we could go sailing tomorrow. I could tell you all about where I've been and what's happened."

There was a brief silence. "Sailing? Okay, Dev. But what about—"

"Cabo would be nice. What do you think about Cabo?" I suggested.

"Cabo? Tomorrow? I'll have to see if I can get some time off."

"Oh, that's right. I forgot. You can't just up and set sail any time you feel like it."

"Well, I'm not exactly a prisoner, but I do have *some* obligations."

"Obligations. Those aren't necessarily bad things. I suppose they're right up there with compromises and commitments." I watched through the glass window as an old man helped his wife out of their car. He took her hand, and they strolled arm-in-arm into the restaurant. "Do you think it's possible to be too free?" I asked.

Craig was silent for a moment. "Are you okay, Dev?"

I thought about the question. Was I okay? I searched my soul for the honest truth. "I'm great. You know, I can wait to go to Cabo until you have the time. We can just putter around the harbor tomorrow and get reacquainted."

"That would be great. I've missed you so much," Craig said, his voice soothing my nerves like a stroll along a quiet, secluded beach.

I watched the old couple from the parking lot find their way to a table. The man helped his wife into her chair, then leaned over and kissed her on the cheek. I smiled. "Me, too. One other thing, Craig—if your offer still stands, then my answer is yes."

I could hear a deep sigh through the phone. I held my breath waiting for his response. "My offer stands for an eternity, Devonie Lace. You name the place and date, and I'm there in a second."

A tiny tear rolled down my face and dropped on my hand. The weight of the world suddenly lifted off my shoulders, and I felt freer than I've ever felt in my whole life.